OUT OF LEFT FIELD

by Ellen Klages

Viking

VIKING
An imprint of Penguin Random House LLC
375 Hudson Street
New York, New York 10014

First published in the United States of America by Viking,
an imprint of Penguin Random House LLC, 2018

Library of Congress Cataloging-in-Publication Data is available.
ISBN 9780425288597

Printed in U.S.A.   Set in Sentinel   Book design by Mariam Quraishi

1 3 5 7 9 10 8 6 4 2

Although this is a work of fiction, the baseball players, politicians, and events of the Space Age and civil rights movement are quite real. The author has used the cities of Berkeley and San Francisco as a setting for the lives of her fictitious characters, and any resemblance of those characters to actual people is unintentional.

Baseball player illustrations by Grant Canfield.

To all the members of the Shazam Club:
past, present, and future.

Chapter 1

Casey on the Mound

"Gor-don! Gor-don!"

The crowd goes wild as the Seals' ace reliever steps out of the dugout and trots to the mound. The bottom of the ninth, two on, two out. Only one batter stands between the Seals and the pennant.

"Gor-don! Gor-don!"

The sound from the stands is deafening. Gordon takes a couple of warm-up tosses, then sizzles one across the plate and nods to the catcher. It's time.

"Burn it over, Gordon!"

"Throw some pepper!"

"Get 'em! Kill da bums!"

"Gordon? Hey, Gordon, you okay?"

I looked up from my mitt, the imaginary announcer's

voice fading. My catcher, PeeWee Ishikawa, stared at me. I nodded. "Good to go."

"You were a million miles away," he said.

"Just waiting for you to give me the signs."

"C'mon, Gordon! Easy out!" Whiz called from the outfield.

At the plate, a skinny kid named Sticks stood with his bat over one shoulder. *Let him wait.* I blew a long, slow bubble of gum, scuffed the dirt with one high-top sneaker, and adjusted the ball, finding the seams, getting the right grip. My side was up by one run, and Mike Bernstein's mother had already called "Dinner!" over the back fence, so this was it. If Sticks struck out, my side would win.

The score didn't matter, much. We played until it got dark—or guys' moms started yelling—and picked up again the next day. Like one endless game, all summer. We didn't have regular teams, either. Most days only nine kids showed up, so we matched fingers to pick, then played four on a side with a pinch hitter. The game itself was everything.

"Let it fly, Gordon!" PeeWee yelled.

I stared at Sticks long enough to blow one more bubble before winding up. My best high leg kick, then a hard slider that broke just before it crossed the plate.

Sticks swung and missed.

"Strike one," Andy Duncan said from the bench. With

a cast on his broken arm, he couldn't hit or throw for beans, so we all agreed he could be umpire. He was pretty good, too. There'd only been one fight, and even then nobody'd gotten punched.

PeeWee lobbed the ball back. It hit the pocket of my glove with a satisfying *smack*. I swiped an arm across the sweat on my forehead before gripping the ball again. A glance over at Mike on first. He wasn't much of a runner. No threat to steal.

"'At's the stuff, Gordon," PeeWee yelled. "Two more, just like that."

"You bet." I pitched from the stretch, a great throw, a blistering fastball that smacked into PeeWee's glove before Sticks could even move.

"Strike two," Andy called.

PeeWee tossed the ball back. I grinned and turned it around in my glove, finding the familiar raised pattern of the stitches. My special pitch. Sticks couldn't hit *that*. Nobody could. I let out a breath, arched my fingers, and wound up into a smooth release. The ball fluttered toward the plate, fooling Sticks into a big, roundhouse swing that missed by a foot. He went around so hard he lost his balance and landed on his butt in a cloud of reddish dirt.

"Strike three," Andy said, and the guys on the field cheered. The boys on the bench groaned and began picking up their gloves and caps and bats.

I stood in the patch of bare dirt that passed for a mound and watched them. It had been a good game, a great finish. Behind me, the setting sun touched the roofs of the houses beyond the outfield fence. I'm five foot two, but my shadow stretched from the mound all the way to home plate. That was about how tall I felt, right then.

"Way to go, Gordon!" a couple of the guys yelled.

I grinned and tipped my cap.

"Nice one," PeeWee said from the backstop. "Can you pitch again tomorrow?"

"Sure." I smiled and thumped my glove. I'd pitch anytime, anywhere.

Behind them, a bell rang, not from the school building, where I'd be starting fifth grade in a couple of weeks, but from the porch of Andy's house, a block away.

"Dinnertime," PeeWee said. "I oughta go."

"Me too," I said. "See ya."

"See ya."

One by one, the guys gathered their equipment and got on their bikes or started walking the few blocks home. Most of us had grass stains on our sneakers and pants, from diving for a grounder. Every one of us was dusted with the red dirt of the infield, cap to Keds.

I tucked the ball into my glove, wedged it under one arm, and walked over to the drinking fountain on the south wall of the school. The water arced high and splashed, and late on a hot August afternoon, it was warm as soup, because the pipes had been in full sun. Better than nothing. I hoped there were sodas in the fridge at home.

"Gordon?" A man's voice, behind me.

"Yep." I turned around.

He perched on the fender of a beat-up convertible parked at the curb. He wasn't old, maybe college age, with a stiff blond crew cut and a blue polo shirt. His arms were tanned, and all muscle. "That last one was something else," he said.

"Thanks. It's my Sunday pitch."

"What was it?"

I shrugged. "Doesn't have a name. It's a combo, a knuckler curve. I'm still playing with the mechanics of it, but it's swell when it works."

"I'll say. How'd you do it?"

"Changed the grip a little. Wanna see?"

"Sure." He hitched himself off the fender and waited while I got my glove out again.

"Look here. If you put your fingertips on the stitches this way—" I held the ball up for demonstration "—it disrupts the orientation of the spin axis, which changes the drag coefficient."

"Whoa. What's your dad, a rocket scientist?"

"Yeah, he is." I was pretty sure that was what he did. I'd only met him twice.

"Go figure." The man shook his head. "Look, kid. I've been playing ball since I was in rompers, but—what the heck did all that mean?"

"It means the ball doesn't have much spin, and so it zigs when you think it's gonna zag." I grinned. "And so far, nobody can hit it."

The man whistled. "Well, you talk like an egghead, but you pitch like a champ. How'd you like to join the Little League? I'm one of the coaches, and we could use an arm like yours."

"Little League? You betcha!" *Zowie*. That was the real deal—official uniforms, a regulation diamond. It was the big leagues, for a kid. "When can I start?"

"Not so fast. First things first. How old are you?"

"Ten," I said, then gave him the whole truth. "Middle of next month."

"Good enough. The league's for boys ten to twelve. This season ends Saturday, but we're holding tryouts for spring teams in a couple of weeks. I think you'll fit right in."

"Sure." *Maybe*. I tugged on the brim of my cap, tightening it down in case my eyes looked worried. I don't have much of a poker face. "That sounds swell," I said, and flicked away a sudden trickle of sweat.

"Something wrong?"

No poker face at all. "Nope," I said quickly. "Just thinking about the Seals. I sure hope they win the pennant this year." That wasn't what I was thinking, but how would he know?

"Going out with a bang, that'd be good," he said, then pointed to my jersey. "You gonna retire that when they're gone?"

"Gone? Whad'ya mean, gone?"

He lifted an eyebrow. "You haven't seen today's paper?"

"Nope. My mom took it to work before I got up."

"Ah. So you don't know." He shook his head and reached onto the front seat of his convertible. "Take a gander, kid. It's gonna be a brand-new ball game in Frisco next year. We're in the majors! First team west of the Mississippi."

He held up that morning's *San Francisco Chronicle.* Its huge black headline read:

Say Hey! They're S.F. Giants Now

"How about *that,* kid?" The man sounded excited.

"I don't get it," I said. "The Seals are a *Red Sox* farm team. Everyone says they'll be in the American League when the majors expand out here."

"That's what I heard, too. But baseball is a business, and it looks like the owners and the politicians have been wheeling and dealing, 'cause the Giants are leaving New York." He scratched his cheek. "That means the

Seals stay bush league, if they stay at all. Can't see why we'd need *two* teams."

No! The Seals were *my* team. They'd played for San Francisco before my *mom* was born. What would happen to Aspromonte and Pearson and Pumpsie Green? I felt my eyes sting, and wiped my face like I was sweaty, to cover. "Look, mister, I need to get home and wash up before dinner."

"I'll bet you're hungry. You played a hard game." He pointed to his car. "Let me get some info from you, and I'll have you on your way in a jiffy." He leaned over and picked up a clipboard from the backseat, then turned around and clicked his ballpoint pen. "They call you Gordon. That your first or last name, son?"

"Last. First is Kay—" *Oh crap*. Fortunately, I stopped myself in time, thought fast, and continued without *too* much hesitation. "Casey. Casey Gordon."

He laughed. "Now, there's a good baseball moniker."

It was. And it really *was* my name, shortened a little. My initials are K. C. I wasn't about to tell him they stood for Kathleen Curie. I was pretty sure he thought I was a boy.

In my dirty jersey and sneakers, I looked like the rest of the guys. Which was fine with me. I'd get to pitch first and answer questions later. It had worked here at the vacant lot. Once the boys saw how I threw, most of them got over the whole girl thing.

"Address?"

I stopped for a sec, because I'd gotten Mom's lecture—more than once—about not talking to strangers. "Can I see that?"

He showed me the clipboard: LITTLE LEAGUE BASEBALL, it said right at the top, with a logo in two colors. That would be hard to fake. So I told him where I lived, and my birth date, September 15, 1947, and my phone number.

"Can I get one for my catcher?" I asked. PeeWee would be over the moon.

"Sure," he said. "He played a fine game, too." He handed me another form and clicked his pen shut. "Tryouts are Friday, September thirteenth, from four until six. Instructions are all there." He pointed to the form, then pulled it out of his clipboard and handed me the carbon copy. "Maybe your dad can get off work and come watch."

I shook my head. "Nope. He lives in Alabama. My folks split up when I was a baby."

"Oh, sorry to hear that." He put his hands in his pockets, like guys do when they don't know what else to say. "Your brother must be a pretty good pitcher, then. He sure taught you good. Where's he play—Berkeley High? College?"

I sighed. I couldn't help it. "I don't have a brother, either."

"Hold on. You're telling me you figured out how to throw a curving knuckler all by yourself?"

"Oh, heck no." I looked up at him. "I learned that from my sisters."

I watched his mouth hang open like he was going to swallow flies. I bit my cheeks so I wouldn't laugh. Not then. I waited until I was a half block away before I started to chuckle.

2

Members of the Club

“I’m home!” I yelled as soon as I jumped off my bike and hit the back steps. “Mom, guess what?” I opened the screen door, expecting to see her sitting at the kitchen table, smoking and doing the crossword puzzle, like most summer afternoons, but her chair was empty. On the table, held down by the salt shaker, was a note:

K—

Co-op meeting.

Home by 7:00. Will pick up pizza.

xoxo—Mom

P.S.: Jules is back.

Jules—Juliana Berg—had been my best friend since kindergarten. In a funny way, she was also the reason

I became a baseball player. Not that she was good at sports—she was short and not very coordinated, except for playing the piano. She was a whiz at that. But last summer, her parents sent her to day camp, and she was only around on weekends. I didn't have anybody to hang around with the rest of the time.

The other girls in my class liked dolls, or jump rope. Boring. One day, wandering around, I saw a boy from my street, PeeWee, playing baseball in a vacant lot. We weren't exactly friends, but we'd played together on our block—Red Light, Green Light and Kick the Can. Those games, it doesn't matter if you're a boy or a girl.

Baseball was different. All boys.

It looked like fun.

I went back every day for a week and watched from across the street. They talked tough and hit each other and got as dirty as possible. I could do that.

"C'mon, easy out! He stinks!"

"You throw like a girl."

Every year since I was seven, my Aunt Babs had taken me to see the Seals play, for my birthday. That June, I started listening to their games on the radio, writing down baseball words and looking them up in books at the library. I figured if I got the lingo down, I could pass. Boys who dropped balls or missed every pitch were allowed, so why not me? I wouldn't play like a girl.

I watched and listened and read about baseball all that

summer. Since I didn't have a dad or brothers to teach me, I asked my sisters for advice. I was the youngest of three girls, but sort of an only child—they were both in high school when I was born. Most of my life, I'd felt like I had three moms. Suze was tall and blonde and looked like a Viking, in a good way. She's an artist. Dewey was a mechanical engineer. She looked a little like Dondi in the funnies, with dark hair and dark eyes. I'm already half an inch taller than her, even though she's a grown-up. She was adopted.

A month before my ninth birthday, Suze turned our backyard into a baseball playground. She bought an old surplus parachute and strung it like a curtain from the oak tree to the garage. That way I could hit and throw as hard as I wanted without the ball going out of the yard, or through a neighbor's window. Again. She hung a rubber tire from a branch for a strike zone.

Dewey taught me about how a ball moves when it's spinning, and how to change that. She gave me a little notebook full of diagrams and explained what it all meant. After another week, I didn't need the numbers. My fingers and my arm had figured out what to do. By the time fourth grade started, the boys at the lot had gotten used to me. They let me stand in left field and catch balls, even hit every once in a while.

Then, *this* summer, Jules went to sleep-away music camp, up in the Sierras, for two whole months. I got serious. I'd grown a couple of inches and was taller than half the boys. By now I could throw a ball where I wanted it, most of the time. About a week after school ended, PeeWee saw me practicing in my backyard, trying to throw a slider.

"You're pretty good," he said. "Lots better than Sherm."

"Thanks." I threw another, that one straight through the hole in the tire.

"Hold on," he said. "I'll be right back." Five minutes later, he handed me a baseball glove. "My brother Eddie's in college now. You can have it."

"Really?"

"Can't play without a glove," he said. "C'mon. Let's check out the lot. A bunch of guys are gone this week, and we could use a good arm."

When we got there, five boys stood around, shooting the breeze.

"Katy can play," PeeWee said.

"I can pitch," I said.

Tony, a sixth grader, just looked at me. "We're not that desperate." He pointed to a flat rock, half-buried in the dirt. "Go stand on second. Try and catch one if it goes that way."

"Like fun," said a pudgy kid named Timmy. "Bet she just falls down and *cries*."

I didn't. Only one ball came in that direction, but I

caught it okay. When it was my turn to bat, I got a hit. A dribbler, but a hit. They next day, I just walked out to second, and nobody said a word.

Richie came back from vacation ten days later. He looked at me and said, "What? Now we let *cheerleaders* on the field?"

"Shut up." Tony stared him down. "You don't want to mess with Gordon."

I grinned all the way to my toes. I was *in*. I wasn't a girl. I was just Gordon. Around the middle of July, they let me pitch a couple of times. By August, the mound was mine.

Jules didn't know about any of that. I could hardly wait to tell her. I got a root beer from the fridge and called the Bergs' number. "Hey. You're back! Wanna come over?"

"Maybe. I don't know."

"What? How come?" I was busting to see her, but she didn't sound too excited.

"My mom's making a special dinner." A few seconds of silence. "I guess I could, for a little while. Daddy won't be home until six thirty. He's covering some meeting."

Mr. Berg worked for the Berkeley newspaper. Jules's mom was a housewife, which meant she cooked and wore an apron like moms on TV. Their house always smelled good.

A few minutes later, I heard Jules come up the back steps.

"Hey," I said.

"Hey."

We stood in my kitchen for what felt like a long time, like we'd just met. Jules looked different. She was tan and her dark hair was longer, pulled back into two little pigtails. She wore a blouse that said CAMP HARMONY above the pocket.

I didn't know what to say first. "Did you like camp?" sounded stupid, the sort of thing grown-ups say when they don't really know you. Jules didn't say anything either. She looked around the kitchen like she was expecting something new and exciting, but it was just our same old stuff.

The Bergs' house was always spick-and-span, everything tidy and just where it should be. My house was messy. Not dirty like garbage, but never really neat. Mom was a professor. Nuclear chemistry. Every flat surface was covered with piles of books and papers. We cleaned off the dining room table for Thanksgiving and Christmas, but the kitchen table was always half-covered with mail and groceries that hadn't gotten put away. A big wooden bowl in the center held keys and pens, rubber bands and paper clips, spare change and a Green Stamps book. There was usually a screwdriver.

Finally I opened the fridge. "Want a root beer?"

"Yeah." Jules nodded. "It's hot." She took a long swig from the bottle. "Oh, that's *so* good," she said. "We didn't have sodas at camp, just bug juice." She smiled at the expression on my face. "It's only Kool-Aid. Made with well water. Lots of minerals."

"Sounds healthy." Her smile made me feel a little better. "So," I said, trying to sound like it was no big deal, "you wanna go up to the attic?"

Jules stared at me, the bottle stopped halfway to her mouth. "Since when are *we* allowed?"

"Since my sisters moved out last month. Dewey finished her PhD and she's in Boston, building robots. Suze has an apartment in the city and teaches art at some fancy girls' school. They gave me the whole attic before they left, with a ceremony and my name in lights and everything. Even a manual for the complicated and electrical stuff."

Jules whistled. "This I gotta see."

We went up the back stairs, then the steep, narrow ones that led to the big attic room—part science lab, part machine shop, part art studio. Bookcases covered two walls, with a window at one end. The other wall—the Wall—was covered with what looked like random junk: a tiny Ferris wheel, model train tracks and pieces of Erector sets, maps, noisemakers, ramps and slides, dolls' heads, pieces of crystal chandeliers, a line of piano keys, a bicycle wheel with jingle bells on its spokes.

My sisters *loved* old junk. Dewey made machines out of it. Suze made art.

When I was little, they babysat me, using the attic as a lab and me as the experiment. I know about things other kids have never heard of: the Greek alphabet and Venn diagrams and how to make paint out of ground-up rocks. Some of it's useful.

"Watch this." I put my soda down and opened the black metal box on the wall. Until last month, the number one rule in my life was that I was never, ever—under *any* circumstances—allowed to go near that box.

Now I could, but it still gave me the willies.

Inside was a panel with four small switches. Typed gummed labels said EAST, WEST, NORTH, LIGHTS. Next to them was a huge Frankenstein-looking lever whose label said ALL. I tugged that one down.

The whole attic burst into lights and sounds. Bells rang, whirligigs whirled, noisemakers clanked, and a row of tiny light bulbs spelled out KATY!

That made me smile. My own private carnival. Jules grinned at me and did a little dance around the room. After a minute or two I pushed the lever back up, and the Wall clicked and clattered into silence. We flopped onto the beat-up couch.

"That is so cool. You can come up here anytime?" Jules asked, as a couple of stray marbles clanged across the bicycle wheel before it finally stopped turning.

"Anytime I want. I'm a member of the secret club now." I stuck my hand in the pocket of my jeans and rubbed the white stone I'd carried for the last month. I showed it to Jules. "It's a magic rock, like theirs. It has its own wooden box, with a lightning bolt on it."

"What alphabet is that, on the rock?"

"Greek. It says *Shazam*. That's from an old comic book. It's short for the names of these ancient guys with super powers—strength and speed and all that. Like Superman, except it's six different guys: Solomon, Hercules, Atlas, and—I forget the others." I shrugged. "Everyone in the club gets their own rock, to show that we stick up for each other, no matter what." I put my rock back in my pocket and looked at her. "I asked them if you could join, too. I mean, if you want." I crossed my fingers behind my back.

"I guess." She shrugged, but her eyes had that sparkly look she gets when she's happy.

"Cool." I nodded. "There is one rule, though. No girls allowed."

Jules stared at me.

"I know. I didn't get it, at first. Dewey said it means that we're not girly girls. We don't squeal when we see a spider, and we think for ourselves. 'Keep asking questions,' they told me. 'Never settle for being ordinary.'"

"I can do that," Jules said.

"Okay then." I reached into my other pocket. "Here's yours. Suze made it so you could join up as soon as you got back."

"Aces." She rubbed her fingers over the letters on the gray stone for a minute, then tucked it into the pocket of her shorts. "Thanks."

Another silence, but this one didn't feel *quite* as weird. We drank our sodas.

"How *was* camp?" I asked after a minute.

"Fun. There was a lake, and bonfires, and scavenger hunts. Also a *lot* of work, practicing every day. And way too many bugs." She showed me the half-healed mosquito bites on her arm. "But—hey! I learned to play the Lone Ranger song," she said. "Turns out it's classical. An overture."

"Go figure."

"Yeah. I was surprised." She drained the last of her root beer and picked up the bottle. "You want me to take this downstairs on my way out?"

"You're going already?"

"I promised my mom I'd only stay a few minutes. My first night back and all."

"Oh. Right. Sure." That weird feeling returned. I suddenly felt like I didn't even know how to say good-bye. I waved as Jules bounced down the stairs.

I stared at the Wall, remembering Jules dancing around, all excited about being up here. I sank back onto the couch. My couch. The whole attic was mine. But it was another hand-me-down.

Baseball was the first thing in my life that *nobody* in

my family had already done. No "Oh, I remember the first time I read that book" or "did long division" or "made scrambled eggs."

I'd really wanted to tell Jules that. About baseball. About *my* summer. Instead I lay there and watched the last rays of afternoon sun slanting through the window, lighting up little bits of dust. It made the attic seem too quiet, too empty.

Chapter 3

Current Events

It was a couple of days before Jules and I finally got to spend a whole afternoon together. We went to the movies at the Elmwood Theater, a double feature—*Attack of the Crab Monsters* and *Invasion of the Saucer Men.* It was fun until a tall kid with a blond crew cut tried to ditch in line at the popcorn stand. He elbowed Jules and his Coke splashed on her pants. He called her a name and one of his friends laughed.

So I stepped, hard, on top of the guy's sneakers.

"Watch your big feet," he said. He took a step toward me, like he was going to try something, but the manager of the theater showed up, his arms crossed, and gave Crewcut a radioactive stare until he and his friends slouched into the theater. That was the last we saw of him, but Jules was all sticky for the whole second show and didn't want to come over after.

Then school started up again. I didn't mind the learning part. I was one of the smart kids and got good grades—except in handwriting. But I hated all the rules.

I couldn't wear my cap. Neither could boys, but at least they got to wear pants. Since June, getting dressed had meant tugging on my worn blue jeans and my Seals jersey and slipping my feet into my high-tops, so perfectly broken in that my feet didn't even notice them.

At school, jeans weren't allowed. Sneakers were out, except for gym. Rules meant nothing comfortable. Only my socks and underpants were the same. I opened the closet door and stared at the clothes on wooden hangers. They looked alien, like they belonged to a kid who'd mysteriously vanished three months ago.

"Katy! Five minutes!" Mom called.

I picked out a white shirt with plain buttons and a red plaid skirt. Pleated, so I could run if I needed to. I laced my new saddle shoes, still bright white, no scuffs. The leather was stiff and tight. *Every*thing felt stiff.

I'd been a kid all summer.

Being a *girl* was for the birds.

Mom sat at the kitchen table with a cup of coffee and a cigarette, reading the *Chronicle.* Next to her was a carton of milk, a box of Grape-Nuts, and a box of Wheaties. Across from her was a placemat with an empty bowl and a glass of orange juice. Mom didn't usually fuss that much for breakfast, but it *was* the first day of fifth grade.

"You look nice," she said. She held up the paper. "Do you want the funnies?"

I shook my head and picked up the box of Grape-Nuts. Wheaties is my favorite—the breakfast of champions—but this morning I wanted a cereal that crunched back. I made it last as long as I could. Finally Mom pointed to the door. "Now or never, kiddo."

"Never?" I put my bowl and glass in the sink.

"Not a chance." She kissed me on the cheek. "Learn something new. Surprise me tonight. I'll make spaghetti."

"I'll try." I liked spaghetti. I picked up last year's blue binder. We'd have to go to the store once I got my school supplies list. Outside the back door, I looked at the bucket of balls, my hands itching to throw a couple, but I didn't want to be tardy the first day.

LeConte Elementary was less than ten minutes down Russell Street, on the other side of Telegraph. Jules met me on the corner of Hillegass. We'd walked to school together every school morning since first grade.

"Hey," she said.

"Hey."

"I hope we don't get Mrs. Lanagan."

"Me too." I made a face. She wasn't scary or anything—not like the junior high gym teacher that PeeWee's big sister called the Dragon Lady. Mrs. Lanagan was just boring. She was about a million years old and talked to kids like we were still babies. Rumors said she put so much powder on her wrinkled face, when she sneezed, it blew all over the first row. I shifted my binder to my other arm. “Maybe we’ll get Miss Hopkinson.” She was young and didn’t mind if learning was fun.

Jules shook her head. “My mom said she got married over the summer and moved away.”

“Rats. Who’s got the other fifth grade, then?”

“I dunno.”

The class lists were taped inside the front door. So many kids crowded around that it was a couple of minutes before we got close enough to see. *Whew*. I wasn’t on Mrs. Lanagan’s list.

Jules was.

“What the—?” I said. “They split us up? We’re not even in the same *class*?”

“I saw.”

We always had been. Jules was one of the smart kids, too, the very best in math, not as good in gym. I found my name midway down the other sheet. Room 120—Mr. Herschberger?

“Mister?” All the teachers were women. The only men were the janitors and the principal. “Jeez. He might be really tough.”

“At least Powder-Face Lanagan is supposed to be a pushover.” Jules shifted her binder from one arm to the other.

"We'll still walk home, right? I'll tell you all about this new guy."

"Sure," she said.

I watched Jules head toward Mrs. Lanagan's room. Crap. *Nothing* was the same this year. The hall was noisy and crowded. Leather-soled shoes squeaked, kids talked all at once, and doors opened and closed. Room 120 was at the end of the hall. A sign said 5-B. MR. HERSCHBERGER.

"Take any seat," the man at the front said. "We'll get organized after the bell rings."

He had a deep voice and was a few years older than my sisters. He had muscles under his short-sleeve shirt, and his brown hair was clipped so close on the sides I could see white scalp through it. He had a bow tie and a clipboard and looked really serious.

Looking around the room, it seemed like the school had mixed *every*one up. A lot of kids had been in the other fourth grade last year, and there were a few I'd never seen before. More than half the class was white, the rest Chinese and Japanese, with five Negroes.

The bell rang.

"Good morning, ladies and gentlemen." His voice boomed to the very last row, and heads all turned to the front. "I am Mr. Herschberger, and this is class five-B." He looked down at his clipboard. "Let's see if everyone's in the right place. Karen Anderson?"

She raised her hand. "Here."

He made a tick mark on his list. "Mike Bernstein?"

"Here."

When he got to me, Kathleen, I said, "Here," and then said, "It's Katy," and he made a note before he continued down the alphabet, stumbling on some of the names: Katsuharo Ishikawa (that's PeeWee) and Magdolina Malinowsky—I didn't even know Madge *had* a different name—and Jimmy "Whiz" Wisniewski, all the way through Pincus "Pinky" Zelizer.

"Very good," he said. He read off names row by row. Karen was in the front by the window, as usual, and Pinky was all the way in the back by the sink. PeeWee and I were in the middle, next to each other. Gordon and Ishikawa. Alphabet neighbors.

Once we were in our seats, Mr. Herschberger handed out a big stack of textbooks—English, Social Studies, Math, and Science. My shoulders ached at the thought of carrying them all home. It might be good exercise, if I didn't strain my pitching arm.

Mr. Herschberger leaned against his desk. "Many of our lessons will come from these books," he said. "You'll learn useful dates and facts and concepts. But we'll also learn from what we observe out in the world." He picked up a newspaper. "For the rest of our year together, we will begin each day with an exploration of current events."

Behind me, a couple of boys groaned.

"None of that." Mr. Herschberger took a step forward.

"I want good citizens in this class. You're too young to vote, or serve in the military like I did in Korea, so *your* job is to be well informed." He looked around the room. "How many of your parents subscribe to a daily newspaper?"

I raised my hand. So did more than half the class.

"Own a television set?"

Every single hand went up.

"Then there will be no excuses. Pay attention to the news. I want you to come in every day with at least one item to share and discuss."

A row behind me, a boy said, "I've got a nifty current event. San Francisco's finally going to get a *real* baseball team!"

What did he mean, real? I started to raise my hand to defend the Seals, when Mr. Herschberger cleared his throat. "Thank you—Mark. I know sports are important to you fellas, but we're going to concentrate on bigger issues."

More groans. He ignored them and held up the *Chronicle*. "I'll take point today. Little Rock. Where is it, and why is it important?"

A bunch of raised hands.

"Yes—" He looked at his clipboard. "Janice?"

"It's in Arkansas, and it's important because of integration."

"Good. What's that?"

"Um." Janice Bailey hesitated, then said, "The high

school is all white, and some Negro kids are trying to get in."

"Are they succeeding?"

"I don't think so."

"Why not?"

"I think they're—"

Janice was interrupted by a Negro girl, one of the new kids. "'Cause the people in that town throwing rocks and calling those kids names—bad names I won't say out loud—and they called in soldiers. With *guns*! Not to protect them kids, but to *stop* them, and that ain't right."

"Excellent, Shirley. We'll work on grammar, and in the future, I'd prefer it if you'd raise your hand before speaking. Otherwise a first-rate answer." He tapped the paper. "Governor Faubus activated the Arkansas National Guard to prevent nine students from entering Little Rock Central High School."

Steve Miller raised his hand. "I thought the law said they *could* go to that school."

"It does, and so does the Supreme Court." Mr. Herschberger stopped for a minute. "The governor believes he is being patriotic. He is upholding the southern way of life, the way things have always been down there. Is he right?"

I raised my hand as I tried to imagine my school surrounded by armed guards. The teacher started to call on Madge just as the bell rang for recess.

We had to line up quietly and march like *we* were in the army, but as soon as feet touched blacktop, all the boys ran over to the grass. The girls walked to the wall and started forming up for jump rope and four-square.

I saw Jules come out of the other door with Cynthia Miller, who'd been in second grade with us. They headed for the swings. I started to wave, then stopped. It felt funny, not being with Jules. But I didn't like Cynthia much—she wore blouses with lace collars—and I didn't *want* to sit and swing today. I wanted to play ball—if the boys would let me. This wasn't the vacant lot. Playground rules were different.

I figured PeeWee'd back me up, so I followed him, glad I'd worn the pleated skirt. When we got to the edge of the grass, a couple of guys gave me funny looks. I pretended I hadn't noticed. I wondered if Mr. Herschberger got the same stares from all the women when he walked into the teachers' lounge.

Everyone lined up behind the rock that marked home plate. "Scrubs!" Mike yelled.

"Scrubs one," Sticks yelled right after him.

"Scrubs two," PeeWee called. He tossed me the ball.

"Wait a sec," said a new kid. Mark or Matt or something. "Why the heck does *she* have the ball? She's a girl."

"She's gonna pitch," PeeWee said. He eyeballed the new kid. "And I'll bet my milk money *you* can't get a hit off her."

He snickered. "You're full of it."

"Here's *my* nickel." PeeWee held out his hand. Behind Matt-Mark, I could see Sticks and Whiz trying not to laugh and give it away.

Matt-Mark shrugged. "Easy money, if you ask me." He held out his own nickel, then crossed his arms, glaring. "Go ahead. Show me your stuff, girlie."

So I did. Recess was only fifteen minutes, not enough time for a real game, or teams, so we played Hit and Run. Get to first and back before the ball got home again, that was a hit.

I went out to the bare patch in the grass. I struck Pinky out first, then Matt-Mark, who looked like steam would come out of his ears. Whiz got a piece of my next pitch, an easy pop-up, straight to Mike. PeeWee hit a low liner and was halfway back to home when the bell rang and recess was over.

On the way back to the classroom, Matt-Mark gave me the stink-eye, but he sat near the front, so he couldn't pull anything funny. Mr. Herschberger tapped on his desk and told us to open our math books, and the rest of the morning was long division.

At lunch, PeeWee used his extra nickel to buy two milks—a white one for his sandwich and a carton of chocolate that he shared with me for dessert.

Chapter 4

Tryouts

Every night before I went to bed, I put a little red X on that day's square of the kitchen calendar, counting down to Little League tryouts. My Gramma'd given me early birthday money, and I used it to go downtown and buy real, honest-to-gosh *baseball* sneakers, with rows of rubber cleats molded right into the soles. I felt like a major leaguer already as I scuffed around the backyard, getting them dirty, breaking them in.

Every day I got up half an hour early to practice before school. I stood exactly forty-six feet from the tire hanging from the oak tree—that's how far a regulation Little League mound is from the plate—and threw my slider and my fastball. I worked on my special curving knuckleball over and over and over, until it went right where I wanted it, nine times out of ten. *That* was the pitch that'd knock their socks off.

Jules had a new piano teacher. She had lessons after school on Wednesdays, and had to practice for a whole hour every afternoon. We still walked home together most days.

"Do you *like* playing with the boys?" she asked.

"I like baseball, and it's their game. Most of them are okay." I looked at her. "At camp, you played music with boys, right?"

"Yeah, but that's different. It's an orchestra, and—" She stopped, right on the sidewalk, and looked at me, then nodded. "Which is *kind* of a team, I guess. Okay. I sort of get it."

That was good. Because PeeWee lived across the street, and he came over all that week after his chores and caught for me, setting up targets inside, outside, high, low, wide, changing it up. I hit his glove with a solid *smack*, no matter what he signaled, then pitched to him so he could practice his swing, hitting line drives into the soft wall of the parachute.

On Thursday the twelfth, I made the last X on the calendar. PeeWee and I worked out until we heard kids get called home for dinner all over the neighborhood.

"My mom says she'll pick us up right outside school tomorrow," he said. "Three thirty sharp."

"Aces," I said. "Make sure she calls me Casey?"

He nodded. "I told her that was your baseball name,

after that poem we had to read for English, 'Casey at the Bat.'"

"That works." I liked that poem. We didn't get a lot of baseball stuff for homework.

I didn't finish my dinner. My stomach was too jittery. Mom looked at me funny, and I said I had a math test at school, which I did, so it wasn't exactly a lie.

I hadn't told her about tryouts. I meant to, when I first got the form, I really did, but she was busy with meetings and classes. Then school started and I had homework and pitching and it kind of slipped my mind. I'd practiced that conversation with her in my head so many times—walking to school, or brushing my teeth—that I almost forgot I hadn't told her for real.

Tonight seemed a little too last-minute. And she taught some seminar on Friday afternoons, so she *couldn't* come and watch. I figured she'd feel bad about that. It would be a much better surprise when I had *news*, when I'd made the team.

I finished my homework and went to bed early. I couldn't sleep. Every time I looked at the clock it was only fifteen minutes later. I guess I finally did, because when I woke up, the sun was coming through the window and it was morning.

The morning of *the* day.

I put my equipment in a paper sack with my Seals jersey and a pair of jeans, slipping the carved white rock into the front pocket. Mostly I left it in its box, because school skirts don't have pockets, but today I could use the powers of those Greek guys.

"Shazam," I said, and felt like Jules and my sisters were rooting for me.

School seemed to go on much longer than usual. I missed two spelling words on a quiz and forgot the capital of Illinois and at the board, I wrote *9 x 3 = 28*, even though I knew it had to be an odd number.

"Something on your mind, Katy?" Mr. Herschberger asked. The class laughed, the way kids do when somebody *else* gets caught, and I felt my face turn red.

The bell finally rang at 3:15. I jumped up and got my sack out of the cloakroom. I walked into the girls' restroom dressed as Katy. At 3:25, skirt and blouse safely hidden at the bottom of the rolled-up sack, Casey walked out into the now-empty hall, in jersey, cleats, and cap.

The tryouts were a couple miles away, at a city field in North Berkeley. I got into the backseat of PeeWee's mom's station wagon and started rolling a ball in the pocket of my glove, fingering the seams, shifting my fingers for each different pitch.

"Sorry, kids. I'd hoped to make some cookies for you," Mrs. Ishikawa said. "But time got away from me."

"There's that bakery on Ashby," I said. "They make good chocolate chips."

She shook her head. "We don't shop there."

I looked at PeeWee.

"Long story," he said.

There was too much traffic for us to stop anywhere else. Mrs. Ishikawa pulled the car into a parking space a few minutes before 4:00 and we got out. "Good luck, Katsu-ya," she said. She kissed his cheek.

"Ma!" PeeWee pulled away. "Guys are *watching*."

She straightened up. "Ah," she said. She smiled at PeeWee, but looked a little sad. "I'll cheer from the seats." She headed off to a knot of other mothers. I saw some of them tugging on shirttails or straightening caps, and more than a few tried to kiss their squirming sons. Maybe it was okay that my mom wasn't here.

I looked around and whistled. It was a real baseball field, the grass mowed short, the dirt of the base paths raked, an actual *mound* with a pitching rubber, the whole shebang. There were two dugouts under the risers of the seats, and a scoreboard in center field.

Maybe thirty boys my age stood around in small bunches, waiting. They burped and spit and popped Bazooka gum and scuffed their sneakers in the dirt—PF Flyers and Keds and high-tops. Only one other kid had cleats. The ones that were far enough away from any grown-ups were loud with jokes and tough talk, like boys did when they were nervous.

"*You're* never going to make it, chimp-face."

"*That* butt-sniffer? Don't make me laugh."

I stood next to PeeWee. The mix of boys was about like our class—mostly white, some Orientals and Negroes. I didn't see any other girls. I tugged my cap down a little and pounded my glove, trying to look like one of the guys. Everyone had a glove. Half the crowd wore jerseys, the rest T-shirts and jeans. Two guys actually had regulation knee-length baseball pants and high, striped socks.

Five men stood around first base, holding clipboards. One of them was the crew-cut college guy who'd scouted me. When the scoreboard clock said 4:00, an older guy with gray hair and a whistle around his neck called out, "Okay, fellas. Gather 'round the plate."

Suddenly, every boy on the field was moving, forming a semicircle in front of the backstop.

"I'm Coach Martin," the man said. He had a strong voice that carried. "For almost twenty years, Little League had been open to *any* boy who wants to play baseball. Your race, your religion, your ethnic heritage—none of that matters. Little League is a true democracy. It does not discriminate in any way whatsoever. Each of you has an equal chance to make one of the teams, based *only* on your skills with a ball and a bat. How about *that*?"

Half the boys gave a ragged cheer.

"That's the spirit." The man smiled. "Today we're going to see how you run, hit, throw, and catch. We'll also be watching for some things that are not so easily measured—healthy competition that includes good sportsmanship and fair play." The other men nodded.

"Success on the field comes from dedication, discipline, and—of course—practice, practice, practice!" He pounded his fist into his hand. "Now, who's ready to *play ball*?"

This time every kid cheered, me included.

"*That's* what I like to hear." He tapped his clipboard. "In order to give you maximum attention in the trials today, we're going to divide you up into four squads." He read off eight names. "You all go stand behind Don."

A red-haired man in gray sweats held up his hand, and those guys peeled off and lined up behind him.

I was in the last group called. Six other kids lined up with me. I smiled. I was taller than five of them. We stood behind the blond guy with the crew cut, who said his name was Coach Dave. He walked out to right field, the rest of us following like ducklings.

We started with running. The hundred-yard dash.

"Step up to the line, tell me your name, and go on my whistle," Coach Dave said. He held up a stopwatch. "I'll record your times."

When it was my turn, I walked up to the line and said, "Casey. Casey Gordon." I'd practiced *that* so many times it came out easy-peasy, like it really was my name.

My time was twelve and a half seconds. Two guys were faster. Swifty was the best, at eleven seconds flat, and Kevin, a beanpole, came in at twelve-two. When the last boy sort of waddled for a whole twenty seconds, I watched Coach Dave frown and scribble on his clipboard.

A high school boy in a BHS jersey tossed batting practice. When it was my turn, I hit two out of four, one a dribbling grounder, one over second base. That wasn't *great*, but was about as good as most of the others. Swifty hit three over the fence, and a stubby guy named Miles hit a rocket back at the pitcher. Kevin hit two good ones, one of them probably a homer.

We got a five-minute water break, then on to fielding. Each of us took a turn in the outfield while the high school kid hit fungoes out to us. Coach Dave watched and made notes.

Fielding's my weak point. A sizzling grounder went through my legs, I bobbled a pop-up but caught the last two. I tried not to smile when Kevin dropped a long fly and also missed a grounder. Then we *all* watched as a kid named Larry Cohen just stood and stared as the ball dropped right at his feet in center field.

"Stinker!"

"Candyass!"

"You play like a girl!"

"Guys." Coach Dave waggled a finger. "I don't want to hear any more garbage talk."

Everyone went quiet. The others took off their caps

to wipe sweat off their foreheads. I left mine on. I knew I didn't *play* like a girl, but even though my hair was pretty short, it definitely wasn't a crew cut.

Coach Dave walked us out to the mound. "Now let's see how you can pitch."

I felt my heart jump a little, and couldn't stop a big grin. Finally. *This* was what I'd been waiting for.

Chapter 5

Sunday Pitch

"Those are exactly forty-six feet away." Coach Dave stood on the pitching rubber and pointed to two tall fence posts at the edge of the outfield grass. Four white cords were strung between them, two across, two up and down, making a square. Behind the contraption was a portable plywood backstop.

"Horizontals are at knee and armpit heights, the bottom and top of your strike zone. The verticals are the edges of the plate." Coach Dave looked from face to face, and everyone nodded.

"Step up to the rubber, take a warm-up pitch—nice, easy tosses, fellas—and go back to the end of the line. After everyone's loose, I'll take a look at your fastballs. You'll each get four tries." He tapped a washtub full of baseballs with his foot. "Any questions?"

"How you gonna measure speed?" asked Sammy, a skinny red-haired kid in a Red Sox jersey. "You got one of them radar guns?"

"Nope. I'm going to stand by the left post, watch for accuracy, and listen to the sound your ball makes when it hits the backstop. It's tryouts, not rocket science." He looked right at me and grinned.

He remembers me! I hoped that was a good thing.

From beside the posts, Dave yelled out "Atta-boy!" or "Good arm!" I was second-to-last in line, so I got a chance to watch my competition. I didn't know if these were the only tryouts, or how many kids the coaches would pick, so I'd been organizing the boys in my head all afternoon—pretty good, no way, need to beat *him*. There were only two of those, Swifty and the tall kid named Kevin. He looked familiar, but I didn't know from where.

Kevin was a lefty. All four of his pitches were lightning fast, and each of them sounded like an explosion against the backstop.

"Strike four!" Coach Dave laughed. "Nice action, Bodell. Nice."

"Thanks, Coach." Kevin thumped his fist into his glove.

"Next!" yelled Coach Dave. "You're up, Gordon."

I picked up a baseball and stood on the rubber, rolling the ball in my glove until it felt like it was part of my hand. I held the glove up to my face, raised my left leg in a high kick, and let it fly. It went through the strings dead center and hit the backstop with a *thunk* I could almost feel.

I threw another, then Coach Dave called, "Give me one on the outside corner?"

"Okay." I adjusted my grip on another ball, and buzzed one that brushed the inside of the left-hand string, just enough to make it vibrate. Then I did it again, on the right side.

"Atta-boy!" Coach Dave said. "Great job." He pointed to the kid behind me. "Last up."

I went back to the end of the line, my arm warm and tingling, trying not to grin *too* much.

"Almost through, guys," Coach Dave said. "Time for your Sunday pitches."

A boy named Scotty raised his hand. "What does that mean?"

"The one you throw when you've *gotta* get the batter out. One he's not expecting."

"Oh. Okay. I can throw a pretty good slider," Scotty said.

"Slider, sinker, curve—if you can throw it, I want to see it. So—" He looked at his clipboard. "Jim Andrews. Step up, name your pitch, let it fly."

Jim was a small blond boy. "Sinker," he said. He stood on the rubber for a minute, fiddling under his glove, then reared back and threw. The ball hit the bottom string and dribbled off into the grass.

"One more."

Most of the boys' special-best pitches didn't do what they were supposed to. Breaking balls went right down the middle, sinkers stayed up in the zone, and more than half the pitches were wild, bouncing right off the poles and rolling off into the weeds. I was surprised—and kind of happy. I tried to be a good sport and not let my face show that.

"Nice try," Coach Dave said, over and over. "Keep working on that one."

But Swifty had a nice slider with some pepper on it, and, naturally, Kevin threw two *wicked* sinkers. I watched Coach Dave tap his pen and scribble on his papers. I hoped he needed more than one pitcher, because Kevin was a shoo-in.

"Gordon?"

I picked up a ball and stepped up to the rubber. "Mine doesn't have a name," I said. "It's a sort of curving knuckleball."

"Oh. That one," Coach Dave said.

"Yep." I closed my eyes for a second, imagining the tire in the backyard as I arched my fingers, found the sweet spot, took a deep breath, and released the ball. It seemed to float in the air, almost no spin, bobbling a little, like a bumblebee flies. It went through the bottom corner of the square opening and hit the backstop with a soft *thunk.*

Behind me, I heard two guys whistle.

"Jesus," said Coach Dave. He shook his head. "Sorry for the language, fellas. That one's—unusual." He looked at me. "Do it again?"

"Sure." I threw another. It floated and bobbled and went through at the same spot, thunking harder against the plywood. When Coach Dave signaled, I gave him two more, one breaking to the right, one right down the middle.

"*That* is one heck of a pitch," Coach Dave said. He clicked his pen and scribbled, and I knew, just *knew,* that I was in.

A couple of kids stared at me. Kevin gave me a frown—not quite nasty, but not friendly, either.

When Coach Dave blew his whistle to end the tryouts, I was as tired as I could ever remember. We'd played longer games at home, but there was a whole lot more sitting in between. Sweat dribbled between my shoulders, and my throat was scratchy and dry.

Another whistle. "Listen up," said Coach Martin, who seemed to be in charge. "You all take ten while we have a parley." He pointed to the benches. "There's lemonade and cups over there, and some of your moms have booned us with cookies."

A big cheer from all of us.

"Help yourselves. You've earned it. Great hustle, fellas."

I trotted over with the others, and found PeeWee. We each downed two cups of lemonade and a snickerdoodle before we could talk. All around us, boys were lying or sitting on the grass, a few of them groaning.

"How'd you do?" PeeWee asked.

"Okay, I think. I bobbled a grounder and whiffed at a change-up, but my knuckler was aces. How 'bout you?"

"Behind the plate, I was solid. Then I hit a liner and blasted one over the fence. But—" He made a face. "You know I can't pitch for beans." He shrugged. "I saw a lot of guys do worse." He ate another cookie. "What happens if we don't make the cut?"

"They put you on a farm team," said a chubby kid. "The Little League minors. There *are* regular games, but no uniforms. You only get printed T-shirts and caps." He leaned back on one elbow. "My brother did it for a year, then got better and moved up. It's not so bad."

His voice sounded like he didn't really believe that last part. PeeWee and I looked over at the coaches sitting in the first row of the bleachers, heads together, tapping pens on clipboards. Another minute and they all nodded. Coach Martin stood up.

"Fellas? Hey, fellas, listen up."

Every face turned toward him.

"I'm going to read off a list of names. If you hear yours,

go stand by Coach Dave over at third base." He looked at his clipboard. "Anderson. Baker. Bodell. Daniels—"

I held my breath, then heard, "Gordon," and let it out with a big whoosh. I was halfway to third when I heard "Ishikawa," too. PeeWee looked over and gave me a thumbs-up. Coach Martin hadn't said which group was which, but since Kevin was already there and Swifty trotted up a minute later, I was pretty sure ours was the In crowd.

By the end of the roll call, I counted fourteen of us with Coach Dave.

"Congratulations, guys. You've made the first cut."

A huge cheer.

"You bet. You should be pleased with yourselves. You played hard and you played well. We'll let you go after some organizational details." He motioned to an older boy who'd been shagging balls back from the outfield all afternoon. "Tom here is the best shortstop in the league. He's twelve, so this was his last season. He's going to show you how a Little League uniform looks, and help me pass out rule books and permission forms."

The boy stood next to Coach Dave. He wore a two-piece flannel uniform—gray pants held up by a leather belt. They ended mid-calf above high red-and-blue socks and a collarless gray jersey with INDIANS in script across the chest. His wool cap was blue with a red bill. He looked *swell*.

"Listen up," Coach Dave said. "We want to take a gander at how you fellas do in a real game before we firm up the team roster for next spring. So a week from tomorrow at noon sharp there'll be a scrimmage game with the 'veteran' ten-year-olds from the season that just ended. You'll need to bring signed permissions if you want to play." He pointed to the uniformed boy, who started handing out booklets and papers, one bundle to each kid.

Coach pointed a finger at me. "Gordon, I'd like you to start, pitch the first inning or two."

"You bet!" I said. I was smiling so hard I could feel my face stretching. I felt like I was floating, or maybe flying.

Kevin gave me a real stink-eye this time. "I seen you somewhere before," he said. "What school you go to?"

"LeConte."

"Oh. *I'm* at Emerson." He made it sound like it was special, but it was only another elementary school.

Before I could answer back, he turned away and loped toward the bleachers. PeeWee's mother came up and grabbed him in a big hug. On the way home, she took us to Bott's for ice cream sundaes.

Celebrating in style.

We were in Little League.

Chapter 6

Take Me Out to the Ball Game

I came home busting to share my news, but Mom was out to dinner with some friends, so I made a sandwich and listened to the radio. The Seals beat the Sacramento Solons and became the 1957 champions of the Pacific Coast League. Not that it mattered much, with the Giants coming.

The next night, Jules slept over, because Sunday was my tenth birthday. In the morning, Mom made us pancakes, with syrup and bacon, and I opened presents. Suze had made me my own baseball card, with my picture and some imaginary stats. She called my "team" the Elmwood Irregulars. I liked that. Dewey had gotten me a Red Sox pennant signed by Ted Williams, and Mom gave me a weird plastic saucer called a Frisbee that could actually fly.

I opened the present from my dad last. Pink paper. I could tell from the shape underneath that it was a book, though, so it might be okay. He always sent a package for my birthday and Christmas, but the older I got, the less he had any idea what I liked. This one was a dud. *A Girl's First Cookbook.* I looked through it, to be polite, but even Mom made a face.

My best present was from my Aunt Babs. Every year she took me to a Seals game in San Francisco. Today's was a doubleheader, and I got to bring Jules along. She didn't give a hoot about baseball, but Aunt Babs was a math professor, and Jules was almost as crazy about numbers as she was about music. Besides, my aunt would buy us as many Cokes and hot dogs as we wanted. Jules's mom only cooked healthy food.

Seals Stadium was one of my favorite places on earth. It sat at the corner of 16th and Bryant and looked like a baseball palace or an ancient temple. A four-story horseshoe, painted mint green, it had a theater marquee with neon lights that said SEALS STADIUM and red plastic letters for today's visitors and game time. Its four light towers were twice as tall as the building. At night, you could see them all the way from the Bay Bridge.

The papers said the Giants were going to build another stadium, south of the city, for the 1959 season. I couldn't see why. Maybe more parking. Otherwise, this one was just about perfect.

Mom drove us into the city and dropped us off at the entrance. She was going shopping downtown, then out for cocktails with people I didn't know. Aunt Babs would drive us home; no one knew when the second game would end.

"Sorry I'm late," Aunt Babs said when she made it through the crowd. She gave me a hug and patted Jules on the cheek. "I swear, everyone in the city is coming to the game today." She was Mom's older sister, which made her fifty-something. She had blue eyes and tortoiseshell glasses. Her brown hair had gray streaks. She lived in a great old house on Russian Hill with her friend Franny.

The crowd was more than half men, in sports coats and hats, some in short sleeves. Most of the women I could see were wearing dresses or skirts, with what Mom called "daytime hats." A few, like Aunt Babs, wore slacks. Not many. She did wear her pearls, though. I was a kid, so I was in my usual baseball clothes, and Jules wore cords and a checkered shirt. We all carried sweaters; even though it was a sunny fall day, if the fog rolled in midafternoon, the stadium would get windy and chilly.

Aunt Babs bought us programs and we went through the gate in the big green cyclone fence that separated the lobby from the ballpark itself. We walked up the wide concrete ramp, slow going because of all the people. Vendors had booths in niches along both walls, selling peanuts and pennants and renting striped cushions for fifteen cents. We got three of those. They weren't only for keeping your butt from the hard wooden seats. When one of the umps made a really bad call, everyone threw them onto the field. Tradition.

We came out of the ramp through the third-base vomitory. I like that word. It just means an entrance in a stadium, but it made Jules laugh. Suddenly we were in another world, all green. The grass was golf-course bright, the outfield fences were dark forest. I stopped and looked and breathed, trying to absorb it, one last time, so I'd never forget. How the dirt of the base paths was raked so neat. The big clock and the scoreboard out in center field. The roaring murmur of thousands of people talking and laughing, and the calls of the vendors walking up and down the aisles: "Hot dogs, get your red-hots here, only a quarter, hot dogs!"

Aunt Babs gave our tickets to one of the short-skirted usherettes, who showed us to our seats, right on the third-base line behind the home dugout. We were so close I could hear the players talking and grunting while they stretched and warmed up.

The stadium was one level, no roof or overhang. Every seat was open to the big, blue sky. Behind us was downtown, seven hills of steel-and-stone skyscrapers. Beyond the outfield scoreboard were the factories of

Potrero Hill. The houses behind them, stacked like stair steps, went up and up and up.

I sat down, put my glove on top of my program, and took a deep breath. I smelled grass and popcorn and the yeasty aroma of bread baking in the Kilpatrick's factory across Bryant Street. On top of the tunnel behind home plate, a band played marches as the seats and the bleachers down both foul lines filled up.

Aunt Babs bought us frosty bottles of Coke and hot dogs with mustard. She sipped at a beer and got out her mechanical pencil to fill in the scorecard when the PA system came on with a crackle. The announcer's voice boomed over the seats with the starting lineups.

"For San Francisco, batting in first position, the right fielder, *Al*-bie Pearson!" The crowd roared with each name, and I watched Aunt Babs enter them: *30 Pearson 9*.

"Okay, *thirty* is his uniform number. I got that," Jules said. "But if he's batting first, why did you write *nine*?"

"He's the right fielder," I said.

"Huh?" Jules just looked at me.

"Okay, the pitcher is one, the catcher is two, first base is three—"

"And right field is last. Got it. There are nine men on a team, right? So that's his *position*, even though he bats first."

"I'll walk you through it," Aunt Babs said as she continued to fill in the lineups for the Seals and the visiting Solons. "It's a fun way to re-create the game in numbers and symbols."

Jules nodded. "Like an equation."

"Exactly. When I draw a line across the—" She was interrupted when the band broke into the national anthem and everyone stood up. Men took off their hats. Ladies didn't have to, but I stuck my cap under my arm, in case people thought I was a boy and was a rude and unpatriotic one.

When the last notes echoed away, the umpire yelled, "Play ball!" and the first Sacramento batter came to the plate. I squinted to watch exactly what our pitcher, Jack Spring, was doing. I had my glove on one hand and my fingers wrapped around the ball I'd brought, trying to figure out what he was going to throw, how to do it. He was a lefty, though, which made it weird.

Every play, Aunt Babs explained the scoring to Jules. She was a good teacher, and since Jules was used to math symbols, she got the hang of it pretty quick. By the third inning, Jules was grinning and making notations on her own scorecard.

Scoring *was* a cool skill to have, full of secret language. A strikeout was a K. Even better, if the guy struck out swinging, that was a *backwards* K. When I listened to the game on the radio, I thought it was fun to fill in all the little squares. But here at the stadium, at a real live game, there was so much to look at, I didn't want to spend time writing it all down.

"Now I see why you like this," Jules said to me. "Sunshine, statistics, and sausages. What a great afternoon."

It really was, I thought, even though the Seals lost the first game. Oh well. They were already the champs, and Sacramento was just trying to stay out of *last* place. I was with two of my favorite people in the whole world, watching baseball on a sunny afternoon that was also my birthday. Being ten was great, so far.

In between the two games, Aunt Babs and Jules went to the ladies' room and the souvenir shop, and I got my ball autographed by Sal Taormina and Albie Pearson and Bert Thiel, who'd once played for the Boston Braves and was my favorite pitcher. The dark blue of the ink looked nice against the white leather and red stitching. A bunch of men in suits or uniforms made speeches. By that time, Jules and Aunt Babs were back with more Cokes and a beer, hot dogs, and Cracker Jack.

The players took the field for the second game. Aunt Babs started to fill in the lineups, then stopped, her pencil in midair. "What the—?"

I looked up and saw Joe "Flash" Gordon, the manager, standing on second base. Albie Pearson was on the pitcher's mound, not in right field. No one was in his usual place.

It was the goofiest baseball game I'd ever seen. Albie

played every single position at least once. The manager pitched, and then got into a beef with the umpire and stormed the plate and started yelling. That was when the umpire took off his chest protector and went to the mound and *he* pitched, in his suit and mask. Even the Solons' manager played as a pinch runner—for the Seals! Everyone in the stands was laughing so loud it drowned out the PA announcer. Aunt Babs gave up trying to score and signaled the vendor for another beer.

We put on our sweaters. The fog wasn't too bad—I could still see the ball when it arced up into the outfield, and I'd been there one night when it completely *disappeared*. The sun started to set, and the windows of the houses across the bay glowed like they were on fire. If I turned around, I could see the Hamm's Beer sign glowing from the brewery across the street. A giant schooner of yellow light, it slowly filled up, topped with white light-bulb foam that overflowed down the side, then drained, over and over and over, bright against the darkening blue sky.

When the last out was called, nobody moved. Everyone in the stadium—more than 16,000 people—stood and applauded the Seals for five whole minutes. Not for the game, or even the championship, but for being San Francisco's home team for more than *fifty* years.

Then it was over.

People started making their way down onto the infield, shaking hands with the players before walking out to center field and exiting through the double doors in the twenty-foot wall that opened at the end of each game.

I stayed in my seat, watching the crowd thin out. In my lap was a paper bag with a brand-new pin-striped Seals jersey, my autographed ball, and the crisp red felt pennant Jules had bought me. Souvenirs of *my* team. Now they were antiques. Relics. The Seals had just ceased to exist.

The Giants would play here next year. San Francisco Giants? How wrong that sounded. My tongue tripped over it every time. San Francisco Seals was so smooth, so—right. A tear ran down my cheek. I wiped it away on my sleeve, then felt a hankie pressed into my hand.

"I thought you'd be happy to have a major-league team here," Jules said. She looked confused.

"Not if it means getting *rid* of the Seals. I wanted them to be part of the majors, not instead of."

Aunt Babs sighed. "It *is* the end of an era, kiddo. I still can't wrap my head around it. I've lived and died with the Seals since I was Katy's age. I saw my first game in 1915, over at 14th and Valencia. They built this place when I was in grad school. I remember cutting a calculus lecture to watch Joe DiMaggio play. Right here. That's a hell of a tradition to let go of."

"I didn't know," Jules said. She slipped her arm through the crook of my elbow and gave me a squeeze. That felt nice.

We walked across the grass toward the center-field gate. I stopped and looked back, one last time, at the green seats, the flags snapping in the wind, the litter of striped cushions.

1957, the year everything changed. My sisters, my class, and now my team.

"Go, Seals," I whispered. I tipped my cap and walked out onto Potrero Avenue, into the cool San Francisco night.

Chapter 7

No Girls Allowed

That whole week, school was a blur. All I could think about was the Little League practice game on Saturday. When the bell rang, I ran home and changed clothes. In my backyard, I practiced every pitch until I could almost hit the tire's strike zone with my eyes closed. Tuesday and Wednesday, PeeWee came over and caught for me; after school Thursday, we finally had enough kids for a game at the vacant lot. Homework, paper routes, and Hebrew school had cut into our roster.

I got a hit my first time up to bat. The "field" seemed so small after the tryouts park, I thought as I stood on the piece of carpet that marked first base. It almost felt like a make-believe game. Come April, I'd be standing on a real pitching rubber, wearing a uniform, playing against kids who were as good as me. I'd still play with

Andy and Sherm, now and then, in the off-season, but they'd be easy outs.

At dusk, I walked home. I loved the feel of my cleats. I walked differently on the sidewalk, striding, a little bit taller. In two days, I'd be a starting pitcher. Life was as swell as swell could be.

Dinner was meatloaf and mashed potatoes, with an apple pie from the bakery. For the first time in weeks, Mom didn't have meetings or an afternoon lecture and had gotten home in time to cook. I sat at the dining room table doing my math homework—long division with *decimals* in it—and the phone rang.

I ignored it. On the second ring, I yelled, "Mom! I'm doing *math*!"

From the kitchen I heard a sigh, then the scrape of her chair on the linoleum, and a soft *chunk* as she picked up the wall phone, midway through the third ring.

"Hello? Yes, this is Mrs. Gordon. No, my husband is *not* available." Silence. "And whom, may I ask, needs to know?"

I put down my pencil and listened.

"Oh. I see." Silence again. And then I heard Mom do something she *never* did. She lied. "I'm afraid you caught me just starting the dishes. Is there a number where I can call you back?" Sounds of scribbling on the pad by the phone. "Thank you. Give me fifteen minutes." She hung up and appeared in the doorway, frowning.

"Do you know a man named Dave Julian?" She pulled a Chesterfield out of the pack in her pocket, clicked her lighter open, and looked at me.

"I don't think—oh." I tried to remember if Coach Dave had ever said his last name. "Maybe. Why?"

"There seems to be a problem with my *son* Casey. A baseball game?" She blew out a stream of smoke. "Something you want to tell me?"

I shrugged. "I tried out for a team," I said, like I did that every day, but I could hear my voice wiggle.

"At school?"

"No. Better. See, a couple of weeks ago this guy Dave saw me playing at the lot. He's a coach, and he was pretty impressed." I rooted around in a pile of papers and found the application form. "I filled this out for you to sign." I frowned. "I'm pretty sure I told you," I said. I tried to make it sound like I'd done my part and Mom had forgotten.

She raised an eyebrow. "And I'm pretty sure you didn't."

Busted. I hadn't. I really had meant to, but it seemed like she was always at meetings, and then I was doing homework and—

Besides, the longer I kept it to myself, the weirder it felt. What if Mom got p.o.'d that I hadn't told her right away? What if she thought "Casey" was a big fat lie, and it was time for one of *those* talks?

She looked down at the form. "Little League, huh?"

"Yeah. Isn't that great? Mom, they have *real* teams and umpires and uniforms and everything!"

"Sounds exciting. And you told him your name was Casey?"

"K. C. Those *are* my initials."

"Yes, I remember naming you."

"Well, if you say it out loud, it sounds like Casey, right?"

"It does. But here, in the space for 'Boy's Name,' you wrote C-A-S-E-Y." She tapped the paper. "Those aren't initials, kiddo."

"It *is* a great baseball name."

"Katy?"

Darn. I knew *that* look. I sat down and fiddled with the fringe of the woven placemat.

Mom looked at me over the top of her reading glasses. "This—Dave—*does* know that you're not a boy, right?"

"He never asked."

"I see." She sighed and read the application again, slowly, then put it down. "Sweetie, this form asks me to agree that my son—not my child, my *son*—can play. You must have noticed that all the language refers to male children."

"Sure," I said. "But I figured it was exactly like a permission slip from school. Those say 'every child should bring *his* lunch,' even though half of us are girls."

"Standard grammar." She nodded.

"Right. So I didn't think it was important. After all, the guy *did* invite me."

"He invited Casey."

"Same difference. He saw me pitch, said they *needed* arms like mine."

"That was him, on the phone. He got a complaint from another parent who claims *Casey* is not eligible to play."

"Of course I am!" I slapped my hand on my math papers. "I threw my heater and my knuckler and ran the hundred in twelve seconds and I made the cut, fair and square."

"Good for you." She tapped her ashes onto a saucer. "Did they give you a rule book?"

"Yeah. I haven't *read* it yet."

"May I see it?"

"Sure." I dug into the pile again and pulled out the yellow booklet. "How come?"

Mom looked at the back of her hand. She'd written some words in ink, like she did when she went grocery shopping. "Section three, paragraph G," she said. "Dave says you're in violation of that rule."

"I haven't even *played* yet. How'm I supposed to have broken a rule?" I thumbed—fast and hard—through the booklet, looking for Section III. "Paragraph—?"

"Paragraph G."

I found it. The world stopped.

My stomach heaved like I was going to puke.

I handed the book to Mom.

"It says—oh. Oh, sweetie."

The paragraph was only one sentence long: *Girls are not eligible.*

I felt Mom's arms wrap around me from behind, felt the scratchy wool of her sweater against my cheek. "I'm sorry, kiddo," she whispered.

"I don't understand! I *made* the team," I said, and heard my voice crack. "I was better than most of the boys. I was *good.*" I felt my eyes sting and rubbed my fist across my face, like I could shove the tears right back in. "It's not *fair*!" I picked up my pencil and snapped it in half.

"Not a bit." Mom smoothed her hand over my hair, the way she used to do when I was little. Then she made a little *huff* sound and stepped back. "This man has *seen* you pitch?"

"He recruited me," I said, snuffling. "And he was my coach at the tryouts."

"You must have impressed him." She handed me a Kleenex.

"I did."

"Maybe he'd be willing to—go to bat for you?" She gave me a little smile and handed me his phone number. "You'll never know unless you try."

I called him back. "Coach Dave?" I said when he answered. "It's Casey Gordon."

"No, it's not." He didn't sound friendly anymore. "You lied on your application, young lady."

"Not exactly," I said. My voice came out small. "My initials really are K. C."

"The K is for Katherine?"

Busted again. "Close." I sighed. "Kathleen. How did you find out?"

"Kevin Bodell saw you at the movies. His mother called your school and discovered that the only fifth grader named Gordon was a girl—Katy."

I almost dropped the phone. *That* was why Kevin looked familiar. He was the rude boy who'd spilled Coke on Jules.

"Son of a b—" I stopped myself. "Coach. You've seen me pitch. You wanted me to *start* on Saturday."

"I know." Now he sounded almost sad. "But there are rules. Any team that breaks them risks losing their Little League sanction."

"Can't you *do* something?"

"Sorry. My hands are tied. If national finds out we let a girl play, all *four* teams could forfeit their field, their uniforms, their sponsors—those boys would lose *everything*. You don't want that, do you?"

Why not? I wanted to scream. *You're taking it all away from me!* I clenched my fist around the phone. "You think *this* is fair?"

I heard a sort of half sigh, half raspberry. "Look, if it

was just up to me, I'd give you a shot. You've got one of the best arms I've seen on a kid your age. If you were a boy, you might make it to the big leagues. But—" He let the rest of his sentence hang in the air.

I waited a minute to see if he was going to finish. "Lemme get this straight," I said. "The *only* reason I can't play is because I'm not a boy?" The B in "boy" sounded like a bomb going off in my mouth.

"That's it." I heard him take a deep breath. "Hey, hey. I know you're disappointed right now. Still, pretty soon, I bet you'll forget all about baseball. You'll grow up, and want to be just like your mom. Am I right?"

"I sure hope so," I said. "You've never met *my* mom." Hmm. I thought for a minute. "Hey, remember when Coach Martin gave that speech about how Little League doesn't discriminate—"

"That's right."

"*—in any way whatsoever*?"

"Hold on. This rule has nothing to do with discrimination," Coach Dave said.

"Oh yeah? Isn't Little League denying *my* civil rights?" I was sorry Mr. Herschberger couldn't hear me.

"Come on now. It's not the same at all. You can still go to the ballpark and watch the games, you—" Then I heard his fingers snap. "Hey, I know. You could be our mascot. Whad'ya think about—"

I hung up on Coach Dave.

I stood in the kitchen, staring at nothing, so mad I could feel my skin shaking.

Mom put a hand on my shoulder. "That was impressive rhetoric, kiddo."

"It didn't work."

"Sometimes it doesn't."

"I hate rules! I hate somebody telling me what I'm *allowed* to do."

"I know. Still, that's—" She stopped, like she wasn't sure if she should say the next part.

"What?"

"That's a big part of organized sports, isn't it? Rules and regulations?"

"I guess." I hadn't thought about it, but it was true.

She gave my shoulder a squeeze. "I think it's time for some apple pie."

"Not for me. I'm not allowed."

"What? And whose rule is *that*?"

"Everyone's." My voice sounded as cold as ice cubes. "If baseball is as American as apple pie, then if I'm not eligible for one—"

Mom stuck out her tongue. "Other people's rules about what girls can and cannot do have *never* applied in this house." She patted my cheek. "Think about it. During the war, your mother helped build bombs—*The* Bomb—and both your sisters own welding torches. You're one of *us*, and I'm proud of you."

I felt my whole body get warm, in a good way. Right then I was glad I had *my* mom instead of some Betty Crocker woman. I sat down. "You know people in civil rights, don't you?"

"I do. Bob O'Leary, one of the fellas on the Co-op board, is a professor at the law school. He's done work for the ACLU."

"A-C—?"

"American Civil Liberties Union."

"Could you ask him about—this?"

"Start at the top, bring in the big guns? Why not?" She looked at the clock. "Still early. I'll give him a call."

Mom talked to her friend for a long time, twirling the phone cord around her fingers in between cigarettes. I couldn't concentrate on long division. Finally she handed me the phone.

"Bob wants to ask you some questions about what actually happened with that coach."

"Okay." I held the black receiver to my ear. "This is Katy."

He asked me a bunch of questions, and didn't interrupt, like some grown-ups. I read him the rule book. Paragraph III-G.

"That's it?" He sounded puzzled.

I turned one page ahead, one page back. "Seems to be."

"Well, it's blunt. No room for misunderstanding." He sighed. "Katy, here's my best legal advice. Write a careful, reasoned letter to their national organization. Explain your skill level and the results at the tryouts. Ask them to consider giving you a provisional chance in regular league play."

"Do you think that will work?"

"Well," he said slowly, "these are rather conservative times. They may not like you rocking the boat." I heard him tap a pen against the phone. "That said, you have nothing to lose by writing that letter—and everything to gain. Who knows? Someone on their committee might actually believe in what they preach about equal opportunities."

"Thanks, Mr. O'Leary." I hung up the phone and sat down again. "He just said I should write them a letter," I told Mom.

"Not a bad idea."

"I guess." I laid my head down on my arms.

After a minute I felt Mom's hand on my shoulder. "Anything earthshaking going on at school tomorrow?" she asked.

"No tests," I said without looking up. "We're just going to finish *The Call of the Wild* and talk about decimals. Again."

"So you won't miss much if you call in sick?"

That got me sitting up real fast. "You'll let me play *hooky*?"

"Both of us. It's good for the soul sometimes. We'll

sleep in, then go out to lunch and talk about this letter. Maybe we can drum up some battle plans."

"Against Little League?"

"Darn tootin'," she said. "Girls in this family don't go down without a fight."

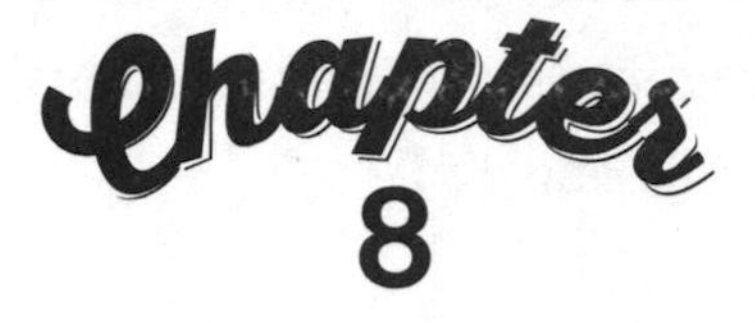

Chapter 8

Fighting Back

I felt a little better after talking to Mom. It was good to have a plan. I went upstairs, but my brain had already started writing parts of the letter, and I couldn't get to sleep. After an hour of turning over and over, I got up and opened the lightning bolt box.

I sat in the window seat, watching the moon between the branches of the oak in the backyard, rolling the white rock in my hand, smoothing my fingers over the carved letters.

Shazam.

No Girls Allowed.

I'd thought that was so cool when my sisters first told me. Welcome to *our* club. No frilly, scaredy-cat, ooh-it's-mud *girls* here. But now—?

How could Coach Dave think I was one of those?

Had he completely forgotten how I pitched?

Why did not being a boy make such a big difference? I didn't always look like a girl, and I definitely didn't *throw* like a girl. Did what was inside my pants really count more than practice and skill?

Not fair.

◇ ◇ ◇

Mom took me to lunch at a place that had checkered tablecloths and waitresses in white uniforms—and really good hamburgers. *Much* better than the cafeteria food my friends were eating today. We talked and scribbled notes on cocktail napkins, and by the time we'd shared a hot-fudge sundae, I knew what I wanted my letter to say. I spent the rest of Friday working on it—wearing my jersey for inspiration. By dinner, I had a lot of it done; pages of cross-outs and piles of crumpled-up paper lay all over the dining room rug.

Saturday morning I scarfed down a bowl of cornflakes and was looking for a fresh ballpoint pen when PeeWee knocked at the back door at half past ten.

"You're not dressed?" he asked. I was still in my PJs. "I figured you'd be outside practicing as soon as it got light." He thumped his catcher's mitt. "I'll wait here, then help you warm up."

I stood there. I'd forgotten PeeWee didn't know. "They cut me."

His eyes got wide, then he shook his head and grinned. "Right. Almost got me with that one, Gordon."

"I'm not kidding."

"Baloney. You blew everyone away. You're the *last* guy they'd cut."

"That's the problem. I'm not a guy." I handed him the rule book, permanently folded open to Section III, and pointed.

"What a bunch of crap," he said.

"Tell me about it."

"It's stupid. You throw better than a *seventh* grader." It was PeeWee's highest compliment. "How'd they find out?"

"That Kevin kid finked. He'd seen me at the movies."

PeeWee said a bad word.

"I know. But I talked to my mom's lawyer friend, and I'm writing a letter to the Little League bigwigs." I pointed to the papers on the dining room table. "I bet they'll change their minds, when they know the whole story. Until then—" I threw the rule book onto a chair. "—it's back to the Elmwood Irregulars."

"That *is* fun," he said. He didn't quite pull it off.

"So, whad'ya say we go start up a game? It's kinda early, but Andy's usually there and—what?"

PeeWee had a weird look on his face. "I can't," he said. "Not today."

"How come?"

"'Cause—I—my—" He looked at his watch. "My mom's driving me to the other game in half an hour."

"You're still going to play?" My voice got loud. "I thought we were pals. All for one and one for all and everything?"

"I—" He stared at his PF Flyers like he was memorizing the laces. "Would you pitch today, if I hadn't made the cut?" he mumbled.

I started to say no, of course not. But it was a lie. If PeeWee wasn't on the team, I'd still take my shot. I frowned. "I dunno. I mean, I was *starting*—at least I thought I was. My big chance."

"Mine too." He put his hands on his hips. "C'mon, Gordon. It's just one game."

"For now."

"You write pretty good. I bet they'll come around before the season starts next spring."

"What if they don't?"

"Then they're jerks." He looked at his watch again. "Look, I should—"

"Sure. Go. Get outta here." I made a *shoo* motion with both hands. "I got better things to do than talk to rats like you."

PeeWee stared at me, then opened the screen door without a word. He let it bang shut behind him and walked away.

I stood there for what seemed like forever, listening

to the kitchen clock tick. Maybe if I never moved again, I wouldn't hurt so much. A car honked and startled me. I went back into the dining room and added a last line to my letter.

Girls have dreams, too.

Half an hour later, Mom came down from her office, carrying some envelopes. "Ready for a second pair of eyes?" She emptied the last of the coffeepot into a cup, slid her glasses down from her hair onto her nose, and picked up my letter.

I paced back and forth from the dining room to the kitchen while Mom hummed and muttered. She grabbed a pencil and made so many changes that I knew if she was giving it a grade, it wouldn't be an A.

Except when she put her pencil down, she was smiling, big-time. "That's *very* good," she said.

"You marked it all up."

"I fixed some—innovative—spelling and rearranged a few bits." She must have seen the look on my face, because she laughed. "No one writes a perfect first draft, sweetie."

"Not even you?"

"Especially me. I'll show you one sometime. Scribbles and second guesses—a complete mess." She took a drink of coffee. "It's an excellent letter," she said. "Solid facts, cogent argument. And heartfelt to boot. That's not an easy triple play."

"Nice baseball lingo."

"I'm learning, too." She picked up the pages and looked at the clock. "Tell you what. I'll go upstairs and type you up a clean copy. Then you can stick a stamp on it and walk it over to the post office before they close."

"Okay." I knelt down to pick up all the crumpled balls. Mom's loafers tapped on the stairs, then a minute later, I heard the different tapping of her typewriter. It sounded like rain on the roof—fast and steady. The floor was uncluttered again when she handed me two cream-colored pages with neat blocks of type, very grown-up and official.

I read it through twice. "Sounds good to me."

"Me too." She uncapped her fountain pen and handed it to me. "Time to sign, seal, and deliver."

"Wow. Really?" Another house rule: I was *not* allowed to use that pen. I took it from her. "How should I sign it? Katy Gordon? My whole entire name? My initials? K. C.—" I made quote marks. "—'Casey' Gordon?"

"Hmm." Mom tapped a finger against her lip. "When I sign checks and other legal documents, I use my real first name, middle initial, and last name. Marjorie W. Gordon."

"You do?" I'd seen Mom's signature, and it just looked like an *M* with a long, loopy bit and maybe an *n* at the end. But okay. I sat down, put the letter on top of a *LIFE* magazine, and very carefully—in cursive that would pass even Mr. Herschberger's inspection—signed my name: Kathleen C. Gordon.

I blew on the ink until I was sure it was dry, then folded the two pages and put them into the envelope. Mom had typed the address of Little League headquarters in Williamsport, Pennsylvania, on the front. I licked the envelope shut, then licked a three-cent stamp and stuck it on. My tongue tasted like glue.

I carried it by one corner and walked two blocks over to College Avenue. As soon as I put it through the slot of the blue mailbox, I felt a tiny bit better.

I'd told the truth. They *had* to listen.

Chapter 9

The Letter

Every day I came right home from school and checked the mail. Nothing except bills and magazines. I got a lot of homework done. On Tuesday, President Eisenhower sent the U.S. Army to Little Rock, so those kids could go to school. That meant there was enough in the papers and on TV that I always had something good for Current Events. It just wasn't the event I was waiting for.

But that Friday, I went in the back door, leaving my wet, leaf-covered shoes on the porch and walked into the living room in my socks. A big pile of mail lay under the slot of the front door.

There it was.

A white business-looking envelope with the Little League logo in the corner. They'd replied *really* fast. I hoped that meant they agreed with what I said, and I'd be back on the team.

Still, my hand was shaking when I set the letter down on the table. I didn't want to open it in my school clothes, dressed like a girl. Upstairs, I put on jeans, then, for luck, my Seals jersey, my cap, and my cleats. I tucked my glove under my arm and looked in the mirror. I looked like a ball player. "I *am* a ball player, and a heck of a good one," I said out loud. I punched my glove, trying to shake the butterflies in my stomach. Then I went downstairs.

I used Mom's letter opener to slit open the envelope. Two pages. Official Little League stationery. I took a deep breath, stirring the butterflies even more, and read it.

> Dear Kathleen,
>
> Thank you for your letter.
>
> The rules which govern Little League play are made by a committee of men who have spent a great deal of time considering the best interests of all young people, boys and girls alike. Since the beginning of baseball as an organized sport, it has always been the sole province of male athletes, and will remain so.
>
> Which is why, as it clearly states in the handbook, Little League is a boy's game,

and girls are not eligible to play, under any circumstances.

There are many excellent reasons for this. First, baseball requires a number of strengths and talents which girls do not possess. Girls do not have the same muscles as boys, and their reflexes are not as quick, so they are likely to suffer injuries to their delicate vital organs. Doctors advise against permitting girls to participate in strenuous activity.

Secondly, the presence of girls would be disruptive and would degrade the game, damaging the boys' natural competitive zeal and jeopardizing their future athletic success. Little League believes that competition builds character in young men. There is no need for that sort of character in young women.

However, if you so choose, there are many roles for girls in the Little League organization. You can join the mothers who volunteer at the concession stands, help decorate the playing fields for special events, or serve as a cheerleader for one of your local teams.

Little League does not discriminate

against girls. Far from it. We are simply protecting them, thus safeguarding our great American pastime and way of life for future generations.

Yours sincerely,
Mitchell K. Grayson
Director, Public Relations

I read it again. I wanted to rip it into little pieces. I wanted to wad it into the tightest ball ever wadded and throw it as far away as I could. I wanted my mom to come home from her stupid lab.

What I finally did was toss it on the kitchen table, pick up my glove, and go outside.

The air was chilly, the backyard covered in damp leaves. I didn't care. I unwound the rope from the iron hook on the side of the garage and stood back as the parachute unfurled with a floppy *whoosh* and a soft thump when its weight sagged the clothesline.

I stepped back to the worn circle in the grass that was my pitching mound and slid my hand into my glove. The smooth leather felt as familiar as my own skin, cradling my hand. The Vaseline I used to keep it supple wafted up to my nose, mixed with the smells of grass and dirt, and I felt like I was home. Not just in my backyard, but where I *belonged*.

Where the man in the letter said I wasn't allowed.

I took the canvas cover off the bucket next to the back door and picked up a ball. I didn't bother with a warm-up, or finding the right pitch. I just *threw* it, as hard as I could, into the parachute.

Thump. The ball hit the silk and dribbled away into the leaves.

Another throw, this one even harder. *Thump.*

My whole body felt like it was vibrating, like I might *explode* if I couldn't throw hard enough. I wanted to *break* something, not thump against a giant curtain. I looked around for another target—and saw the little window on the side of the garage. I knew that would shatter. I'd done it before, by accident. This was different, but—this *was* different.

I curled my hand around another ball, turned toward the window, and cocked my arm, my leg raised—

A bigger hand wrapped around mine.

"Save your allowance, kiddo," Mom said in a soft voice. "Try a couple of these. They do the trick for me."

I turned around. Mom held out a cardboard carton of eggs.

"Eggs?"

"They break, every time." She took the baseball out of my hand and replaced it with an egg. The white oval was cold against my skin.

I frowned, then shrugged. *What the heck.* I lobbed the

egg at the trunk of the big oak. It hit with a *crack*, and yellow yolk ran down the grooves of the rough bark.

"It helps if you yell," Mom said. She handed me another egg.

I turned around. She looked serious. *Okay, then.* I turned back and cocked my arm. "Stupid Little League," I said, louder than normal. The egg cracked a few feet higher up on the trunk.

"Better?" Mom asked.

"Not much."

"Yell louder." She handed me another egg.

So I did. Each throw was harder, and each time I yelled I felt my insides let go a little bit. With the sixth—or maybe seventh—egg, I yelled as loud as I have ever yelled in my whole entire life, louder than cheering for the Seals. I yelled a word so bad that I'd never even *whispered* it before.

All Mom said was, "*That*'ll give the neighbors some cocktail conversation." She passed me another egg.

When the carton was empty, my throat felt like raw hamburger. I stood there, my hands curled into fists, shaking like there was an earthquake inside me.

"C'mere, sweetie." I felt Mom's arms wrap all the way around me, and she walked us backwards to the wooden steps of the porch. She sat down, pulling me into her lap, her legs on either side of me. Her hand brushed across my cheek, then she kissed the top of my head and began to rock me, like she did when I was a baby, sort of singing, a tune with no words. *Ba-ba-bum, ba-da-bum, ba-ba-bada-ba.*

I leaned back against her sweater, smelling cigarettes and Ivory soap, and closed my eyes. The sound and softness and Mom-ness surrounded me like a nest. I stopped fighting the tears that had been waiting since I read the letter, and I cried.

When the hard, sobby part turned into sniffles, I felt the glove slide off my sweaty hand, replaced with a cotton hankie.

"Blow," Mom said.

I did. A long, honking half sneeze, half loogie that left my ears ringing and the hankie sopping.

"I read the letter," Mom said after a minute.

"I figured." I blew my nose again, then wadded the hankie in my hand. "What do you think?"

Mom moved her legs and stood up. "I think my behind is getting cold, and we should continue this in the kitchen, with some cocoa."

"Okay."

I sat at the table while Mom fussed at the stove. I picked up the letter. "It's not fair," I said.

"No, it's not." She stirred the pan. "Delicate vital organs, my ass. It's the worst kind of ignorance." She pitched her voice lower and sounded like my school principal. "That's the way it's always been, and we don't want to hear about anything else." She opened the cupboard.

"That's what Mr. Herschberger said about the governor, in Little Rock."

"It's an apt analogy." She handed me a steaming mug. "Same principle."

I blew on the cocoa. It was too hot to drink yet. "The students—the Negro ones—they kept trying, right?"

"Yes, they did."

"So if I fight Little League, can I *make* them change?"

"Maybe, maybe not. The people in charge don't seem at all interested in your very cogent arguments." She took a sip of cocoa. "And I'm afraid that, in your case, asking the president to send in the army is not an option."

"What if we hired your friend—Mr. O'Leary? What if we went to court and a *judge* made them?"

"It's not that simple." Mom sighed. "Little League would have dozens of lawyers. The case could drag on for years."

"*Years*?"

"'Fraid so. Even if you won—and frankly, I think that's a long shot—by the time there was a decision, you'd be too old for Little League."

"Are you saying I shouldn't even *try*?" My voice sounded tiny, and shocked. I could feel tears prickle the edges of my eyes again.

"No. I would never say that." She reached over and

patted my hand. "If you decide to sue the bastards, I'll back you all the way. But—" She stopped and shook a cigarette out of the pack in her pocket and lit it with a snap of her silver lighter, blowing the smoke in the direction of the back door. "—you need to be sure it's what you want."

"I am."

She held up her hand. "Not so fast. There are consequences to any action, and we need to talk through a few of them."

"Like what?"

"I'm going to order a pizza." She reached for the phone. "It's going to be a long conversation."

Chapter 10

Mom's Story

She ordered a medium pepperoni for delivery, then hung up the phone.

"What did you mean—consequences?" I asked again.

"For starters, how do you feel about spending the next two years wearing a dress and your good shoes and sitting very quiet and still most of the time?"

"Yuck! No way."

"I didn't think so. But that's what talking to lawyers and judges requires. After school, in the summer, all the times you could be outside, playing baseball with the neighborhood kids, you'd be in an office or in court."

"That sucks eggs."

"Yep. And let's imagine you're on your way into the courthouse and crowds of total strangers start yelling at you and calling you bad names."

I stared at her. "Why would anyone do that?"

"You're challenging the status quo—that's Latin for keeping things the way they are. 'Good' girls don't behave that way. And the sacred sport of *base*ball?" She started to pace across the kitchen, gesturing with her cigarette while she talked. "Wanting to change *that*—" She made her voice low, and loud this time. "—why, it sounds un-American to me. Are you a communist, kid?"

"What? No," I said, annoyed. "That's ridiculous."

"Maybe. But you've read the headlines."

"I don't—" And then all those mornings of Current Events flashed through my brain. Pictures of people in Little Rock yelling and carrying signs: INTEGRATION IS COMMUNISM, JIM CROW IS THE AMERICAN WAY!

"Oh."

"See. Not as simple as it sounds." She sat down and stubbed out her cigarette. "Let me tell you a story."

"This isn't where you tell me that I'm growing up, and pretty soon I'll be a young lady, and I'll find out that sewing is *just* as much fun as baseball, is it?" I folded my arms across my chest and scowled.

"God, no!" Mom burst out laughing. "I skipped 'young lady' as often as I could. Ask your gramma." She went to the fridge, opened a beer, handed me a Coke. "But this *is* a story about me."

"About when you were my age?"

"No, a lot older. I was forty. It was the summer of 1950. Your sisters were still in high school. You were not quite three."

"Okay." I didn't remember much from that far back. "What happened?"

"The university asked all its professors to sign a 'loyalty oath.' They wanted me to swear that I was not now, and had never been, a communist or a member of any group that wanted to overthrow the government. Several dozen of us refused to sign."

"Why? *Were* you a communist?"

"No." She leaned against the counter. "But I believe in freedom of speech. And thought. And freedom to associate." She waved her hands. "The whole Bill of Rights." She paused. "You know what that is?"

"Uh-huh. Mr. Herschberger talks about it a lot."

"Good for him. What I *also* believed was that being forced to sign that oath was wrong."

"Because they were trying to keep that status quo thing?"

She smiled. "Exactly."

"Like Little League."

"Close enough."

"So you did the right thing."

"I stood up for what I believed, yes."

"Good for you!" I pumped my fist in the air. "And you won, right?"

"No. That's what I mean by consequences. The university fired me. They fired anyone who wouldn't sign." She bent her head to light another cigarette, and I saw that her hand was shaking. When she started talking again, her voice sounded like *she* might cry. "I lost my job. I lost my lab and my security clearance, and had to stop all my research."

She looked at me, straight in the eye. "I also lost a few friends. And it ended my marriage. Your father filed for divorce a month later."

"Because you wouldn't sign some stupid paper?"

"Phil and I had been at odds for a long time. The oath was merely the last straw. You know where he works?"

"At the rocket place, in Alabama."

"Yes. He was still in New Mexico then, but it was—is—a top secret project. Having a wife who'd been blacklisted—that was what they called it—could have jeopardized *his* security clearance."

"Would he have lost his job, too?"

"He never had to find out. He made very sure I was legally at arm's length." She puffed on the cigarette, then made a face and ground it out in the ashtray like she was squashing a bug.

I sat there for a minute, not knowing what to do or say. I fiddled with a ballpoint pen, clicking it in and out, thinking about what she'd said. Finally I asked, "You're still a professor. That means you *did* get your job back?"

"Yes. The courts finally decided in our favor. But it took three years—three years of not being allowed to do what I love best. Even now, I'm barred from ever working on classified projects again." She reached over and squeezed my hand. "That's what I mean about consequences."

"It was worth it—right?"

"I don't know, sweetie. I honestly don't."

I was quiet for a long time. I'd never had a conversation like this with a grown-up. My head felt achy from trying to think about all of it, about what I was supposed to do next. "Are you telling me I *shouldn't* try and fight Little League?"

Mom stood up and wrapped her arms around me. "I want you to do what you think is right—always. But you're my baby, and I don't ever want to see you get hurt."

"That's not a very good answer."

"I know. I'm sorry. It's a difficult question and—"

The doorbell rang. The pizza guy. Suddenly, I was starving. Mom picked up her purse and went to the front door, coming back a minute later with a cardboard box that smelled *so* good.

We'd each wolfed down a piece before I said, "So what would *you* do?"

"I can only offer you the same advice I gave both your sisters—more than once. You have to pick your battles."

"What's that mean?"

"It means that sometimes it's a waste of time to beat your head against a wall that will never move. Even when you're right." She picked a piece of pepperoni off a slice in the box. "There are lots of different ways to fight."

"Like what?"

"Like—" She drummed her fingers on the table. "Like, how many boys play in the neighborhood game with you?"

I counted on my fingers. "Nine or ten regulars."

"And all of them know you're a girl, and that you can play baseball as well as they can."

"Better," I said.

Mom laughed. "Okay, better. That means that—simply by playing in a vacant lot—you've changed their ideas about what girls can do."

"I guess."

"It's a start. One boy at a time."

"That'll take *forever*. What can I do *now*?"

"Do you think Little League is wrong?"

"Of course!"

"Then you need to look for ways to prove that." She took a long drink of beer. "It's not going to be instant, kiddo. Or easy. Trust me. I've been through this with both your sisters."

"They never played baseball."

"No, but Dewey tried to take mechanical drawing five times—five different years, four different schools—

before she succeeded. Because *those* classes were only for boys. And Suze has butted heads with what girls are *supposed* to be like her whole life."

That was true. "Okay." I swallowed the last of my Coke. "I think I need another one of these. My throat's kinda sore from outside."

"I can imagine. You did some fierce yelling." She gave me a funny look, as if half her mouth wanted to smile and the other half was trying not to. "May I ask where you picked up your salty vocabulary?"

"It happens, when you play with boys."

Chapter 11

Think Like a Scientist

Saturday lunchtime I called Jules. We walked to school every morning, but since she was in a different class all day, and had to practice piano every afternoon, I felt like I hadn't seen her in a long time. And I really needed a friend.

"Wanna come over?" I asked. I crossed my fingers.

"Okay. Can we mess with the Wall? I have an idea."

"Sure."

Fifteen minutes later, she was at the back door with a paper sack under one arm. "I can only have fun for a little while," she said. "My mom says I have to be home by two, because we need to go to Hink's to buy me new shoes." She made a face. "On a Saturday."

"Your mom," I said, shaking my head. We got glasses of milk and some Oreos and went up to the attic.

"What's your idea?" I asked.

Jules grinned and opened the paper sack. Inside was a kid's xylophone, one end of the wooden part splintered to pieces. "The bars already have holes, so I figured we could hang them up with string or wire and they'll make neat sounds when the marbles roll down and hit them."

"Cool," I said. "There are tools on Dewey's shelf."

Jules found a flat-head screwdriver and started prying up the smallest bar, which was painted bright red. The paint was already chipped.

I watched her for a minute or two. "You're good at solving puzzles and stuff."

She nodded without looking up.

"Wanna try to help me with one?"

"Math or science?" she asked.

"Baseball."

Jules rolled her eyes. "What is it this time?"

"I told you Little League sent that awful letter?"

"Yeah."

"You wanna hear exactly what they said?"

"Sure." The red bar popped off the end of the xylophone into Jules's hand. "That's one." Jules smiled. She slid the screwdriver under the orange bar. "Go ahead."

I read her the letter. When I was done, her face looked like she'd just eaten lemons. "That's a *whole* bunch of hooey," she said. One end of the orange bar screeched up. "Isn't it?"

"I think so. But I don't know how to *prove* it."

"What would Dewey do?" Jules asked. She pulled the other end of the bar off the wood with her fingers.

"That's a good question." I sat down on the floor and stared at the Wall. I could almost hear Dewey's voice, explaining how things worked, soft and patient. She'd taught both of us how to solve problems like a scientist. But this was baseball, not physics.

The attic was quiet for a few minutes, until Jules pried the yellow bar off the xylophone and it hit the floor with an *almost* musical clang. "Well?" she said.

"Okay. I know with the scientific method I need to find facts that don't fit their hypothesis." I looked down at the letter. "They claim that it's harmful for girls to play baseball. But since I don't know beans about muscles or vital organs, I'd probably need some important doctor and tests and reports to prove that part wrong."

"That would be complicated," Jules said. "Read me the first part again. About the beginning of baseball."

I did.

> Since the beginning of baseball as an organized sport, it has always been the sole province of male athletes, and will remain so.

"*Sole* province? That seems kinda unlikely," Jules

said. "You can't be the *only* girl in the history of ever who's played baseball. *Ouch!*" She pulled a splinter out of her thumb. "That part should be easier to prove."

"You're a genius, Berg. There must be a list of women baseball players *somewhere*—if there are any."

"Other than Katy Gordon, Girl Wonder?" Jules teased.

I stuck out my tongue and walked around the room, to Dewey's desk, then to Suze's. I opened drawers, flipped through a couple of cut-up magazines, looked at pictures, ran my fingers along the shelves of books. The attic was full of books about science and math and art, not sports. Mom's books were all about chemistry. I thought about my room. I did have a couple of Chip Hilton baseball books, two Seals programs, and last year's major-league yearbook. But if there was *anything* about girls—or women—I'm pretty sure I would have noticed. Where else could I—?

"Bingo!" I said.

"What?" A big green xylophone bar hit the table.

"The library. I've got to go to the library."

"Now?"

"As soon as you finish that. You have to leave in half an hour anyway, right?"

"Shoes," Jules said with a big, dramatic sigh.

We ate the rest of our Oreos, and I helped Jules get the last bars off the xylophone.

"Call me if you track down that list?" she said when it was time to go.

"Really? *You* want to know more about baseball?"

"Now it's like a mystery." She shrugged. "I'm curious what clues you'll find."

"Okay. Sure." I followed her downstairs and got my library card.

I've been reading since I was four, and had my own card before kindergarten. That was *way* younger than the rules said, but the head librarian was used to my sisters and made an exception. Starting last year, I didn't even have to stay in the Children's Room, and was allowed to check out as many books as I could carry, even though the sign said three at a time. Three books? That was barely enough for one rainy weekend.

I jumped on my bike. The neighborhood library was only a few blocks from my house, but it was pretty small. The main library downtown had almost every book ever published, along with dark, twisty shelves called "stacks" that had copies of really old magazines. I might have to go there, and it was more than a mile away.

The Claremont branch looked like an English cottage outside. I stuck my bike in the rack and went in. It's one of my favorite places, cozy and warm, with wooden floors and bookshelves, and stained glass reading lights on big oak tables.

I started with the card catalog, natch. Two inches of cards about baseball—*BASEBALL, rules, BASEBALL, organization*—but at the end of the alphabet, nothing under W for *BASEBALL, women.* I tried G for "girls," and even F for "female" and L for "ladies." Zip. I wrote down the shelf numbers for baseball—mostly the 796s—and went into the nonfiction room. I spent half an hour pulling books off the shelf and looking at tables of contents and chapter titles and indexes. Nothing.

I looked over at the reference desk. Mrs. Wentworth wasn't my favorite librarian—I didn't think she approved of children touching the big important books—but she knew where to find everything. I took a step in that direction, then stopped, and if I hadn't been in a very quiet library, I would have snapped my fingers.

I *did* know where to look.

In a little alcove was a table that held two shelves of dark-green volumes, each twice as thick as a phone book. *Readers' Guide to Periodical Literature.*

For me, they were the best part of the whole entire library, like my secret playground. I'd never told anybody that, not even Jules or my sisters, because I figured it probably crossed a line into Too Weird. I loved the *Readers' Guide*. They had lists of every article published in almost every magazine since the beginning of time. Okay, back to 1890, which is about the same thing. Maybe there hadn't been enough women baseball players for a whole book, but if they existed at all, there *must* have been magazine articles.

The dates were stamped in gold on the wide spines. Some of the volumes were so big I'd have to use both hands to get them off the shelf. I started with the very first one, to make sure I wouldn't accidentally miss anything. Besides, if women had played baseball in the last couple of years, I figured everyone would know. Even my *mom* would know.

I opened the first, skinniest volume—*1890–99, A–K*—and took a deep breath. Ancient paper. It's maybe my second-favorite smell—right after the leather of my glove—musty and dry, because the pages were from the olden days. I felt like I was hunting for treasure.

I turned to the Bs. Only a few entries. Either there weren't many magazines back then, or baseball hadn't gotten popular yet. I dragged *L–Z* down and tried under "Sports," and "Women," just in case, then moved on into *this* century.

By 1910–14, the book was thicker, and BASEBALL took up three full pages. I read as fast as I could. I didn't really know what I was looking for, just hoped a line would pop out, that I'd know it when I saw it. I found articles that sounded interesting, but not useful—like "Baseball and the City Urchin," in the June 1911 issue of *Collier's*.

I sighed. Urchins wouldn't help me. I kept looking. In 1919, I finally found a promising category—WOMEN IN

SPORTS, but all it had underneath the bold part was "*see* SPORTS FOR WOMEN." So I did, my fingers flipping pages as fast as they could. Jeez. Only *one* article? About tennis?

My arms were sore and my eyes were getting tired by the end of the 1920s. The type was tiny and close together, all abbreviated, like *SciAm J 139:40 Jn23.* All those initials and numbers meant that I had to keep stopping to puzzle things out, which was slow. By the 1930s, each volume was more than six inches thick, and when I pulled the next one down from the shelf, it was almost too heavy to lift.

I was about to give in and leave the rest of the 1930s—and the '40s, and '50s—for Monday after school when I struck gold.

BASEBALL players, Women

Girl who fanned Babe Ruth.
LitDigest 109:41–3 Ap18 '31

Chapter 12

A *Literary Digest* Emergency

My heart jumped in my chest, like I'd touched a light socket. There it was, in black and white. Proof.

I wanted to whoop and punch my fist in the air, but kids who made a ruckus in the library got thrown out. Instead I wrote down the information and tore off a tiny piece of notebook paper to mark the page, so I wouldn't have to hunt for it again. I put the book back on the shelf, then walked—okay, maybe bounced—over to the reference desk.

An old lady in front of me asked way too many questions about the succession of the British throne, and was Charles II before or after Oliver Cromwell? I wanted to scream that it *wasn't important anymore!* I didn't do that, either. I took deep breaths and shifted my weight from one foot to the other, like I do when I'm waiting for the batter to get settled, and when the woman was *finally* satisfied, I stepped up to the desk.

Mrs. Wentworth gave me one of those fakey grown-up smiles. "Hello, Katy. What brings you here on a Saturday?"

"I need the—" I looked down at what I'd scribbled. "—the April eighteenth issue of *Literary Digest*. From 1931."

She looked startled and stared at me for longer than I thought was actually polite, then said, "Well. Let me see if we keep back issues here." She opened a big binder with alphabetized names of magazines, each with numbers beside it. "Homework?" she asked while she ran her finger down the list.

"Sort of." I watched her finger and crossed my own behind my back. *Be there, be there, be there,* I whispered without moving my lips.

"Sorry," she said. She closed the binder. "You'll have to go downtown for that one. All we have from 1931 are *Time* and *LIFE*."

Rats. I looked at the clock. Ten after four. "How late is it open today?"

"Until five, but Periodical Room requests have to be in fifteen minutes before closing. Unless your mother drives you, I don't think you'll make it."

Double rats. "When do they open tomorrow?"

"Oh, they're closed, dear. Tomorrow is *Sunday*."

Triple rats.

My face must have looked like one of those urchins, because Mrs. Wentworth made a sort of *tut-tut* sound and said, "Do you need it before school on Monday?"

I didn't, but I also felt like I would explode if I had to wait two more days. It's wrong to lie to a librarian, but this was an emergency. I nodded, as slow and sad as I could.

"I suppose I could call over and see if they can pull that volume for you. That will save you a few minutes. You might just make it." She reached for the phone. "Go on, scoot!"

I scooted. Maybe Mrs. Wentworth was okay. I rode my bike as hard as I could, standing up on the pedals the whole way, taking side streets to avoid traffic lights, and made it to the corner of Kittredge and Shattuck in record time. I raced into the lobby, sweaty and breathing loud and hard, and when I looked at the clock, it was only 4:30.

The Periodical Room was downstairs. I took the steps two at a time, and when I hit the floor, the librarian at the desk looked up. "Are you Katy Gordon?" she asked.

"Yes. Ma'am." The words came out in little huffs.

She smiled. "I can't say I've ever seen such an urgent need for *Literary Digest* before." She patted a large yellow-brown book. "Here it is. All I need is your library card."

I gave it to her and carried the volume over to a reading table. It thumped a little when I put it down, and a man sitting at the next table scowled at me. "Sorry," I whispered.

Literary Digest came out every week. All bound together, it was hard to tell when one issue ended and another began. I finally found April 18th. The cover had a picture of Abraham Lincoln. I pulled the crumpled scrap of paper from my pocket. The pencil was blurry from my sweat, but I could still read it. Page 41. I flipped through pages of neat old ads—Packard cars and Spud cigarettes—and suddenly, there it was.

THE GIRL WHO FANNED BABE RUTH

Her name was Virne Beatrice "Jackie" Mitchell, and she was a pitcher! There was even a photo of her, because she'd pitched an exhibition game against the Yankees. And she *struck out* Babe Ruth *and* Lou Gehrig. Back-to-back.

Jeez-sooey! If *that* wasn't proof enough for Little League, I didn't know what was.

I started to copy the article. The library closed in ten minutes, and I'd never be able to write that fast. I took the open book up to the librarian. "I need to make a copy of this article, please."

"It's ten cents a page." She looked at the clock. "Oh. We don't take requests after 4:45."

"Please, ma'am? *Please?*"

"It's that important?"

"It really is," I said. "My whole future depends on this."

"I see." She thought for a minute, then winked at me. "In that case, I suppose we can bend the rules a little." She took the book into a back room where I couldn't see, and came back a couple of minutes later with three sheets of chalky gray paper. "That's thirty cents."

"There was a third page?"

"Yes. It only had a few lines on it, but I thought you'd want the whole article."

"I do, but my allowance is only twenty-five cents." I dug into my pocket, pulled out the quarter Mom had given me at lunch, and put it on the desk.

"Hmm." She tapped a finger on the papers. "That last page wasn't worth a whole dime, if you ask me." She took the quarter and gave me back a nickel. "And photos don't come out very well on our machine."

They didn't. Jackie Mitchell was a fuzzy gray blur. The print part was readable, though, and it had all the facts I needed. "Thank you!" I said.

"You're welcome, dear." She smiled and put a wooden CLOSED sign on top of her desk.

I folded the pages and tucked them into the back of my jeans, where they wouldn't flap while I rode.

I sang "Take Me Out to the Ball Game" at the top of my lungs most of the way home.

Jackie Mitchell busted their stupid hypothesis into smithereens.

Chapter 13

More Digging

"Mom! Mom!" I dumped my bike on the grass and ran up the back steps, pushing the door open. "They're wrong! I found one!"

She looked up from her crossword puzzle. "One what?"

"Baseball player. A professional *girl* baseball player!"

"Really?" She put down her pen. "Where?"

"At. The. Library," I said. The words came out separate because I was trying to catch my breath. I flopped onto one of the kitchen chairs. "Her name is Jackie Mitchell, and she *struck out BABE RUTH*!"

"That's impressive. What team is she on?"

"None now. She's from 1931, and she played for—" I pulled the article out and unfolded it. "—the Chattanooga Lookouts."

Mom frowned. "I'm not a baseball expert, by any means, but I've never heard of them."

"Minor-league team. There are a lot of those. And it was only an exhibition game, before the season actually started. Still, Mom—Babe Ruth!" I bounced in the chair, then got up and got a Coke from the fridge and drank half of it before I sat down again. "*And* Lou Gehrig."

"Really?" She held out her hand. "Let me see."

I gave her the article. "It's not a very good picture of her, on account of the machine at the library can only make gray."

"The copier in our department isn't much better," Mom said. She read the pages quickly, pausing to tap her fingernail on a couple of sentences, saying "Hmm" and "I wonder" before she put them down.

I burped, from drinking the Coke so fast. "'Scuse me. Wonder what?"

"This article cites two other primary sources—oops, research talk. I mean it mentions two newspaper articles. I wonder if they'd have any more information on this—" She looked down. "—Jackie Mitchell."

"The *Readers' Guide* only lists magazines. But if I'm going to argue with Little League, it would be good to have *all* the facts."

"True." She tapped her fingers again. "It just so happens I work for a rather large university with a great many resources. Would you like some assistance?" She raised an eyebrow and lit a cigarette.

"You'd do that for me?"

"Nope." She waited for a second, blew a smoke ring, and then said, "I'd just get you in the door. You'll have to do all the work. Good research skills are a secret weapon that will come in handy down the road."

"Secret weapon. Cool." I thought for a minute. "Do you have to teach on Monday afternoon?"

"No, just budget meetings all morning."

"If I ride my bike to school, I can get to campus by three thirty. I could meet you."

"Do that. Doe Library. By the card catalog."

◇ ◇ ◇

I'd always liked the main library on the UC campus. It was the biggest building I'd ever been in—except for Seals Stadium, and that was mostly outside. The card catalog room was a wood-paneled, shelf-lined place about as long as a football field, with a high, high ceiling. It was very quiet. The only sounds were papers shuffling, a few people whispering, and the soft thumps of the wooden catalog drawers opening and closing.

The bells of the Campanile tower outside had just rung the half hour when I saw Mom come in at the far end of the room. She was dressed like a professor today—tweed skirt and a cardigan sweater—and carried her brown leather briefcase. The heels of her lady shoes clicked on the marble floor of the big room, echoing a little.

She kissed me on the cheek. "I made some phone calls at lunch," she whispered. "The newspaper room has the 1931 Washington and New York papers cited in your article. I asked them to pull the first week in April for you."

"They'll do that? I'm not even a student here."

"No, but I'm a professor, and that comes with a few perks." She pointed to a door at the other end of the room. "It's downstairs."

At the desk in the newspaper room, Mom showed her faculty ID to a boy in a Cal letter sweater, and he wheeled a metal cart over to one of the polished wooden tables. With a grunt, he lifted the biggest book I had ever seen in my life. It was dark green, about three feet high, two feet wide, and a few inches thick. As big as our coffee table. The boy eased it down and slid it across the wood.

"Lemme know when you need the next one." He went back behind the desk.

"Good luck, kiddo," Mom said. She pulled today's paper out of her briefcase. "I'll be over there with the crossword. Raise a hand when you're done." She brushed her fingers across the back of my head and left me to deal with the giant book.

I had to stand up to get it open. The spine said *New York Times* in black letters. Inside were whole newspapers, bound on their left sides. I stayed standing and turned the pages, carefully, so I wouldn't make noise or, worse, tear one. I found the sports pages and read. Nothing. I turned about forty more pages just to get to the next day, and there she was, on April 3, 1931.

Jackie Mitchell.

It was a different picture. She wore baseball pants and a letter sweater. I sat down.

The headline read:

GIRL PITCHER FANS
RUTH AND GEHRIG

This article was longer and had a lot more details than the *Literary Digest* one. I dug in my school bag for a pencil and started to write down the facts. After a minute or so, I heard the desk boy behind me. "Miss?" he said. "We can make copies, if you want."

"Really? It's so big."

He shrugged. "We're used to that here." He gave me a handful of thin paper strips. "Mark the pages with these."

"Thanks." I put the paper strip near the bound edge.

For the next hour I read old sports pages in three different newspapers. Desk Boy was sweating by the time he hauled the last one over. By now I knew the dates I was looking for, and could scan the pages pretty fast.

Then I gasped, out loud, which made everyone in the quiet room look up from their reading and stare at me.

"Sorry," I whispered.

Mom got up and came over. "What did you find?"

"The commissioner of baseball." I looked down at the page. "Kenesaw Mountain Landis. He voided her contract a couple of days after she pitched." I looked up at Mom. "Does 'voided' mean he *fired* her?" I tried to ask it in a whisper, but I was maybe a little loud, because I was mad.

"Sounds like it." She sat down. "Keep reading."

I did. I stared at the page. "He said that baseball was too strenuous for a girl to play. Even though she struck out Babe Ruth?" I sat back in the chair, disgusted. "That's exactly what Little League said in their letter."

"That doesn't make it true," Mom said softly. "Maybe this Jackie fought back."

"Maybe, but—" I looked at the page again, marked it with a paper strip, and sighed. "If she got fired after only one game, do you think she counts?"

"I don't know. One woman, one game might not

break their hypothesis, but it definitely puts a crack in it." She patted my shoulder. "Sweetie, you've only just *started* looking. I told you it wouldn't be easy."

I clenched my fists and wanted to hit something again. I was already p.o.'d at Little League, and now I was p.o.'d at all of baseball, at stuff that happened years and years ago. I wanted to talk to Jackie Mitchell, to ask her about it, but she was probably dead. Wait—was she? I did addition in my head. If she was seventeen in 1931, she'd be—hmm. Only forty-three now. That was even younger than Mom.

I looked up. "Are there phone books here? For other cities?"

"I think so. Why?"

"Maybe Jackie Mitchell still lives in Chattanooga."

"Worth a try." She smiled. "Excellent reasoning, kiddo. Are you done here?"

"For today."

We stopped at the desk, and she told the boy to make copies of all the flagged pages. "Bill it to the chemistry department, this account." She wrote some numbers on a piece of paper.

"Sure, Professor Gordon," he said. He looked over at the pile of huge books, now bristling with paper strips, and sighed. "I'll have them ready tomorrow."

Mom nodded. "Call my office."

We went upstairs to another room, this one full of phone books. I found Chattanooga's from last year. And sure enough, there she was.

"You're lucky she never married and changed her name," Mom said while I wrote the information down.

"Do you suppose if I send her a letter, she'll answer?"

Mom picked up her briefcase. "Only one way to find out."

Chapter 14

A New Moon

I spent a couple of days writing a long letter to Jackie Mitchell. There was so much I wanted to know. I thought about calling her on the phone, but that was long distance and really expensive. And what if she hung up? What if I got all tongue-tied? A letter was a lot easier.

I asked her when she started playing, and how did she get a contract for the Lookouts? Were there any other girls on the team? What happened after the commissioner fired her? Did she keep playing? If she did, where was that, and could she tell me more?

I addressed it to Jackie Mitchell, Girl Pitcher, in case the address I had was for the wrong Mitchells. I figured the post office would be able to find her, because she *must* be famous in Chattanooga. I walked to the post office and mailed it after school on Thursday.

I'm not very good at waiting, so while I walked home, I figured out what to do next. At dinner, I told Mom my plan. "Now that I have proof about girls and baseball, I'm going to write Little League another letter tonight, and tell them they're *wrong*!" I hit my hand on the table, and my fork bounced onto the floor. I picked it up. "Sorry. I'm excited."

Mom didn't say anything, just took a bite of stew.

"What?"

She patted her mouth with a napkin before she answered. "Want my advice?"

"Do I have a choice?"

"Always." She sat back, lit a cigarette, and watched me through the smoke.

After a minute, I sighed. "Okay, what would you do?"

"Wait until you hear back from her. She'll probably have a lot more information for you. You want your next letter to have as much ammunition as you can muster."

I thought about that, and frowned. "But I want to do something *now*."

"I know. Patience has never been a family trait." Mom put down her coffee cup. "Tell you what. I'll go upstairs right this second and get you a file folder. You can start organizing your research, and keep those copies from getting any more tatty."

"That's a good idea. It might end up as *legal* evidence of them being wrong."

"You never know."

She came back a few minutes later and handed me a stiff manila folder. I unfolded the newspaper articles and the gray copy of *Literary Digest* and laid them flat inside. On the little tab I wrote GIRL BASEBALL PLAYERS, in case there were more than just Jackie and me.

◇ ◇ ◇

Friday was sunny, and after school there were finally enough guys for a game at the lot. PeeWee and I hadn't talked to each other since he went off for the Little League game. For more than an hour, I pitched, and he caught, but we just threw the ball back and forth, no chatter. All business. I pretended like I didn't notice, but I saw that Sticks and Andy did. That could be a problem. If the other guys had to pick sides, me or PeeWee, I'd bet they'd suddenly remember I was a girl, and I'd be on the outs again.

PeeWee lived across the street from me, so after the game ended, it wasn't weird that we walked home on the same sidewalk. We'd gone about a block before I got up the nerve to ask him, "How'd it go at the—other—game?"

He looked startled. "It was okay," he said. We crossed Telegraph Avenue. "I tagged that kid Kevin out. Knocked him *hard* with the ball."

"Good," I said.

"Yeah." Another half a block, then he said, so soft I almost didn't hear him, "You know of any Japanese guys in the big leagues?"

"I don't think so. I hadn't thought about it."

"I have. A bunch." He stuck his glove under his arm and shoved both hands into his pockets. "Maybe I'll be the first. That's why I went ahead and played."

"Oh. Okay." I sure knew how *that* felt. "Sorry I called you a rat."

"Yeah." We passed by four more houses before he asked, "So, we're jake again?"

I stopped and thought about it. "I am if you are," I said. I buddy-punched him in the arm, and he punched me back, and that was good.

When I walked in the back door I heard typing from upstairs. "I'm home," I yelled.

"Dinner at six thirty," Mom yelled back. I ate a few Fritos, just to hold me, and looked at the TV listings in the paper. At 8:00 there was a brand-new show, *Leave It to Beaver*, about a kid my age. That sounded pretty fun.

I worked on my book report—*The Enormous Egg*—about a boy who hatches a dinosaur by mistake. Mom came down and started heating up leftover stew. She turned on the radio, KPFA. If you ask me, they play too many folk and classical songs, but even I sang along to "This Land Is Your Land." Mom, too, tapping her fingers on the counter.

We'd gotten to the part about the redwood forests when an announcer's voice interrupted. "We have just received word that scientists in the Soviet Union have successfully launched a satellite that is now orbiting the earth. This small artificial moon, called Sputnik, is a magnificent achievement, a milestone in human history, and a great step in the exploration of the universe.

"Listen now, for a sound that will forever separate the old from the new, the first broadcast from outer space: *beep . . . beep . . . beep . . . beep . . . beep . . .*"

Mom stared at the radio. It beeped once every couple of seconds, over and over. That sounded creepy, like a Saturday-afternoon sci-fi movie. She turned the dial. The beeps were everywhere. Even KOBY, the rock-and-roll station that Mom *never* listened to, went from Elvis singing "Heartbreak Hotel" to *beep . . . beep . . . beep.*

We ate in the kitchen, then sat and listened for hours. I didn't even notice I'd missed that *Beaver* show. Mom and I just stared at the radio. Every single channel had news about Sputnik.

"Why do we call it such a weird name?" I asked her.

"*We* didn't name it. The announcer said it's Russian for 'traveling companion to the world,' or something like that."

"Can we play gin while we listen?" I asked. It wasn't as much fun as Monopoly or Sorry!, but it was a game Mom would play. I'm not very good at just sitting still either.

"Sure thing, kiddo." She rooted around in a kitchen drawer and found a deck that had all fifty-two cards.

We played for about an hour, the radio guys telling about how this was the beginning of the Space Age, and how the world had changed forever. All the men that were interviewed were scientists, and they sounded excited, even though it was the Russians who did it, and not us. Then again, everyone knew KPFA was lefty.

I watched Mom deal the cards. "What do you think about all this? As a scientist."

"I believe in expanding human knowledge," she said slowly, "and this is a stunning achievement." She lit a cigarette. "I'm just wary of what will happen next. Politics is bound to rear its ugly head. And I'll bet dollars to doughnuts your father and his crew are having hissy fits about being beaten to the punch."

She drew a card, rearranged her hand for a minute, then laid it all down. "Gin," she said. "Let's call it a night."

I went up to bed and got into my PJs, but I just lay there, thinking about all the stuff on the radio. Was it good—because it was science? Or was it bad—because the scientists were Communist Russians? The enemy. Why did nothing in Current Events ever have an easy answer?

◇ ◇ ◇

"Katy. Wake up, kiddo."

I felt Mom's hand on my shoulder and opened my eyes. It was still dark outside. "Whaz—?" I sat up and rubbed my eyes. "What time's it?"

"Four thirty in the morning," Mom said. "Put your shoes on and come with me. You can stay in your PJs."

"Huh?" I figured this was a weird dream, but when I pinched myself, it hurt. "How come?"

"You'll see."

I got out of bed and reached for the lamp. Mom put her hand over mine. "Don't. No lights. You don't want to lose your night vision." I found my sneakers by touch. She led me through the hallway and down the stairs to the front door, opening it quietly and stepping out into the yard.

When we got to the sidewalk, I was surprised to see lots of the neighbors standing around with mugs of coffee, or sitting on lawn chairs, like the Fourth of July parade was about to come by. Some of them had binoculars, and Mr. Dawson had set up a telescope. To my left, a mile away, the Campanile on campus was lit up, looking sort of like the Washington Monument.

"What are we waiting for?" I whispered.

"The Space Age," Mom said.

We sat on the curb, the concrete cold through my flannel PJs. I could see a fraction of light gray to the east when a man two houses down said, "There it is!" He pointed up and toward the northwest.

I lay on my back and looked up at the stars. The Big Dipper and the three-point belt of Orion the Hunter—and then I saw it, up *way* higher than an airplane. A glowing blip that was *moving.* Not zipping across like a shooting star, but gliding like a single tiny headlight in far, far away traffic.

"That's Sputnik," Mom said, lying next to me. She reached over and held my hand. "You're seeing history with your own eyes."

All around me, conversation had stopped. Everyone was looking up, watching the sky in silence. In awe. Me too. My mouth was open, and I tried to make myself believe what I was seeing. It didn't feel real. Something was *up* there, in the sky, with the stars that had been there forever. For the first time—ever—Earth had two moons.

All the planets and the constellations had Greek or Latin names: Jupiter, Cassiopeia, Ursa Major. Ancient names for an ancient sky. This one was different. Sputnik. It sounded like science fiction, like the future, not the past.

Somewhere to my right, I heard a click and a hum as one of our neighbors turned on a transistor radio, and as I watched the little blip move, my arms went all goose bumps.

beep . . . beep . . . beep . . .

Chapter 15

Yom Kippur

I went back to bed, and by the time I got up and dressed it was time for lunch. I could hear Mom in her office, talking on the phone, so I made myself a peanut butter sandwich, left her a note, and headed downtown to the library.

I'd been there enough that now the librarians recognized me, and one of them, Miss Sherman, usually helped me out when there were no grown-ups in line. That first Saturday in October, she asked if I'd heard of Babe Didrikson Zaharias.

"Sure. Everyone has." She'd won gold medals in the Olympics a long time ago, and was maybe the most famous woman in sports, even if it was mostly for golf.

"Well, one of the patrons just returned her autobiography. Since you're interested in women athletes, I set it aside for you. Here."

"Okay. Thanks." I sat down at the reading table and skimmed through the Olympics part, and then—zowie!

She'd played in the *major* leagues. Only for exhibition games, in spring training, pitching for the Athletics and the Cardinals. But that's the American League *and* the National League. Hardly any *men* had done that. She also pitched for a team called the House of David. Mom was right. I definitely needed to find out more. I made some notes, then closed the book and headed to the *Readers' Guide.*

I had to look back through the 1920s and '30s again, because I was looking for different subjects, but I did find a couple of articles. The library only had one of the magazines. I spent another week's allowance on two gray copier pages with a fuzzy picture of baseball players with long hair and beards. They were all men, and it was some kind of church team. The article didn't mention Babe, but at least I had some new information for my folder, and new clues to follow. Better than nothing. I'd just pulled the 1941 volume off the shelf when lights in the library flickered off and on. Ten minutes before five. Miss Sherman shooed me out, but stamped the book first so I could take it home and read the rest of it.

Mom was in the kitchen, KPFA on the radio, of course,

and was actually *baking*. "Where have you been?" She sounded a little mad and pointed to the clock. "It's twenty after five!"

"So? I said I was going to the library."

"We need to be at Gramma's before sundown."

"Tonight? Do I have to? I've got a book I *really* want to read."

"Not a chance. Mama's made a big dinner." Mom frowned at me. "I told you on Monday. Do you even listen?"

"Sorry," I said. "I guess I forgot." She probably *had* told me. I'd been thinking about Jackie Mitchell. "What holiday is it?"

"Yom Kippur. The end of the Jewish New Year."

"In *October*?"

"It's a completely different calendar. Based on the moon *and* the sun."

"So what year does Gramma think it is?"

"5718." She was almost smiling again. "I suspected you'd ask, so I looked it up."

"At least it's got fifty-seven in it, like the ordinary year," I said. We were Jewish, but not as much as the Bergs. The religion passed down through the moms; since Gramma Weiss was, Mom was, so—technically—I was, too. The only time it came up was holidays at Gramma's. Otherwise no one in my family paid much attention.

The timer on the stove dinged. Mom opened the oven

and put a glass dish on the counter. Cinnamon-scented steam rose from a crispy, golden-brown casserole.

"That smells great," I said. "What is it?"

"Noodle kugel," she said. "I haven't made one in years, but Mama was in temple all day and asked me to help out." She looked at the clock. "Go up and change. We've got to go."

"Do I have to dress *up*?"

Mom shook her head. "She said you should feel comfortable. Put on a pair of nice pants and tuck in your shirt and you'll do."

"O-kay." I changed and tucked, and sighed, because it was a *weekend*, and all I wanted to do was lie on the couch and read.

Gramma's house was fifteen minutes away, north of campus. I sat on the front seat of the Rambler, a towel on my lap under the hot noodle thingy, trying to tell Mom about what I'd found at the library. She wasn't really listening. The car radio was tuned to KPFA, too. All the news was still about Sputnik, but they'd started playing some songs in between.

"Margie!" Gramma was waiting in the front hall. She was the only person in the world who called Mom that. "Is it true?"

"What, Mama?"

"The Communists. They've put a baby moon up there?" She pointed to the ceiling.

"That's what the radio says."

"I watched the TV news last night, but I had to turn the set off for Shabbat."

"I know." Mom kissed her on the cheek. "Where do you want this?"

"In the kitchen, on the counter." Gramma looked at the door. "Where's Suze?"

"In the city, where she lives. It's a Saturday night, and she's worked hard all week."

Gramma made a *tsk-tsk* noise and waved her hand. "At least my Katy is here." She kissed me, twice, and I smelled face powder and hair spray. "Come. As soon as we've said the prayers, you can help me with the latkes. Sundown's in a few minutes."

"Sure thing!" Latkes were one of my favorite foods. They're supposed to be for Hanukkah, but Gramma makes them for me on all her holidays.

She had invited three other widows from her temple—Mrs. Stein and Mrs. Melman and Mrs. Kushner. They all stood around the dining room table, waiting. Gramma lit a candle, and they said Hebrew prayers and drank wine so sweet they even let me have a taste. When the ceremony part was over, Gramma and I went into the kitchen. She did the hot-oil frying part, and when she put the latkes on a cookie sheet, I patted them with paper towels—for the grease—then used the spatula to move them to the nice-china platter. She made around twenty, and I was starving by the time dinner was served.

That was beef brisket and latkes, with green beans, which are *not* my favorite, but are better than peas. There was a little more praying, and then all the grown-ups talked about the satellite and the beeps. They didn't have any new information, only opinions, and those were loud. I was bored until dessert. The noodle thing Mom made was so good I had seconds.

Old ladies go to bed even earlier than most kids, so we were home by 8:30. I'd just settled in to read about Babe Didrikson for a while when the phone rang. My dad, calling long distance from Alabama. It was almost midnight there, so it must be an emergency, or at least important. It wasn't my birthday or Christmas, and since he wasn't Jewish, he probably didn't even know it was a Gramma holiday.

Mom talked for a minute or two before she started frowning. She handed me the phone. "Your father says he'd like to tell you the *real* story," she said, and snapped her lighter open.

"About Sputnik?" His job was so top secret I wasn't sure what he actually *did.*

"What else?"

I held the phone to my ear. "Hello?"

"Katy. How're you doing with all this news?"

"Okay, I guess." It always feels a little strange to talk to him. He's kind of like someone on TV. Familiar, but not really part of my life. "We'll have *lots* for Current Events in school Monday."

"I'll bet you will." He cleared his throat. "You know that I'm in Huntsville, working with Dr. von Braun? He's the best rocket scientist in America."

"Uh-huh."

"Well, you can tell your class that *our* team could have launched a satellite two years ago."

"*That* would have shown the Russians. Why didn't you?"

He made a grumbling sound. "The White House gave the funding to another program. A mistake. We had the superior technology."

"Why didn't they—?"

"Eisenhower doesn't trust Wernher, er, Dr. von Braun. Old news, a holdover from the war." I heard him blow out a puff of air, and wondered if he was smoking his pipe. "This Russian stunt caught us all with our pants down, but we've got men in Washington right now, briefing the president. We'll be up and running in no time."

"What are you going to call it?"

"What?"

"Your baby moon. Does it have a name?"

"Not yet. The project does, but—" I heard him chuckle, far away in Alabama. "—that's top top secret. I can't even tell my little girl. But I'll phone you when we're ready to launch. How about that? The biggest news of the year, and you'll be the only fourth grader to know."

"I'm in *fifth* grade."

"Oh. Right. Right." He puffed again. "Still, I'll bet *that*'ll impress your teacher."

"Probably. When's it going to be?"

Silence. "A month. Maybe two, depending on how long the paperwork takes. Down here, we're raring to go."

"That's good."

"You bet'cha." Silence again. "Hmm. I should probably let you get ready for bed. Promise me you'll set the record straight with your teacher? Tell her we may have lost the ball on the twenty-yard line, but we're going to *win* this game, leave the Russkies in the dust."

"Him. My teacher is Mr. Herschberger."

"Oh? Is that right? Even better. He'll understand." He said goodnight and then the phone was all static. I hung it back on the wall and sat down.

"Gung ho, hooray for our side?" Mom asked.

"Pretty much." I leaned against the kitchen door. "What did Dr. von Braun do in the war?"

Mom blinked, then made a sour face. "Short version? Or professor lecture?"

"Short, please. I want time to read before bed."

"He built rockets for Hitler. V-2s. The Germans used them to bomb London. They killed more than four thousand people."

"He was a *Nazi*?"

"In a nutshell." She got up and poured a cup of coffee. "Look him up at the library sometime."

"Maybe I will." *That* would shake up Current Events.

Chapter 16

What Goes Up . . .

It seemed like the whole world had changed that weekend.

Monday morning, the sidewalk and the hallways buzzed with conversation. Some boys talked about the Braves, who had tied up the World Series in game four, the Yankees fans backing up their arguments with baseball cards: "Yeah, but Mantle hit .365 in the regular season and Hank Aaron only got .322—"

I'd listened to the game on Sunday afternoon, but I kept walking. They let me pitch at recess, but that wasn't the same as butting in on boy-talk in the hall.

And even the World Series came in second to space. *Every*one—boys, girls, teachers, the janitor—was talking about Sputnik.

It wasn't very big—it weighed 184 pounds and was

the size of a basketball. It circled the entire earth every ninety-six minutes. All those facts had been in the paper. It was what we *didn't* know that had everyone wondering.

"Those beeps gotta mean *some*thing. Probably a secret code."

"My dad says the Commies are using it to spy on us."

Sputnik had bumped everything else off the news. A lot of it didn't make any sense to me. Friday night, when Mom and I first heard about it on the radio, Sputnik was all about scientific achievement. By the time school opened, the papers made it sound like we were at war with the Russians—and they were winning. Politicians in Washington called it a menace, as bad as the attack on Pearl Harbor, and asked the president to declare a national week of "Shame and Danger."

All of a sudden, everyone sounded scared, not excited.

Current Events took all morning. I shared what my dad had told me and got a check mark in Mr. H's book for extra effort. Andy got one, too. His dad worked at one of the labs on campus, and his news was that the Russians had exploded a huge H-bomb as a test. He said they could use Sputnik to drop one on us, anytime they wanted.

"*My* dad says *this* one's already brainwashing us from outer space, so we'll all turn into Commies," said Timmy Lawton. He'd worn a tinfoil hat to school, because it bounced the Russian rays right off. Mr. H made him throw it away.

"I've got a bigger bombshell," Pinky said, holding up the paper. "The *Dodgers* are moving to Los Angeles."

He was a lot more excited than he'd been about anything the Russians had done. That kind of made sense. The Russians had been on our side during the war, but the Dodgers and the Giants had been sworn enemies for more than fifty years. Mike raised his hand and said that Hank Aaron had hit a *three*-run homer in the World Series and—

Mr. H held up his hand. "Stop. Even this week, sports are not Current Events."

Lots of grumbling. Even more when we went on to long division.

The front page of Wednesday's *Chronicle* had the first picture of Sputnik. It didn't look like much—a silver ball with four antennas coming out of the back, like toothpicks stuck in an olive—but we spent an hour talking about it. When the recess bell rang, twenty of us huddled around PeeWee's transistor radio, listening to the ball game. The Yankees won, tying the series again.

Game seven started at one o'clock on Thursday afternoon in New York. That's only ten in the morning in Berkeley. I could barely sit still, waiting for morning recess. We listened for fifteen minutes, and when the bell rang, nobody wanted to go back to class. But nobody wanted detention, either.

At 12:35 that afternoon, I heard yelling in the hall

outside our door. Mr. H stopped reading from the list of spelling words. "What on earth?" he said. He walked outside and was gone for less than a minute. When he came back, he took a radio in a leather case out of a drawer and put it on top of his desk.

"I am going to make an exception to my rule," he said, turning it on. "History is made in many ways. Our national pastime has stretched beyond its original eastern boundaries. Milwaukee won." He smiled.

Half the class cheered. Most kids who followed baseball had a favorite team, even if it played in another city, far away.

"Milwaukee's not *west,*" Pinky said with a sneer. "But San Francisco sure is. As far west as you can go. It'll really be the national sport when we get a team next spring."

We already had one, I thought. The Seals. I didn't say that out loud.

Mr. H let us listen to the radio until recess. Cheers and pandemonium, two thousand miles away. On the playground, a few boys had radios, and baseball cards were out on the blacktop. I didn't really *get* baseball cards, but even I could see that all of a sudden, Hank Aaron and Warren Spahn were like gold. A fourth grader tore up his Mickey Mantle and dumped the pieces into an empty milk carton. Andy had the only Lew Burdette, and when KNBC announced that Lew was the World Series MVP, that made Andy an automatic captain for the afternoon game.

After a couple of days, World Series fever died down. Baseball season was over for the major leagues, and mostly for our after-school games, too. It got dark earlier and earlier, and there were lots of rainy, chilly days. I didn't put my glove up on my closet shelf, but there wasn't much chance to use it, even in the backyard.

Sputnik fever didn't go away. Every day the *Chronicle* printed a map showing the flight path over America. Mr. H worked Sputnik into every lesson—math problems, science, even history and spelling. He taught us about the Russian Revolution and how they became Communists. We learned about the Chinese inventing rockets, how planets orbit the sun, and what a parabola was.

"This is a standard flight path." He drew an arc on the chalkboard. "But this month, for the first time in human history, an object went *up*, and didn't come down."

Madge raised her hand. "On Sunday our pastor said godless communists shouldn't control the heavens," she said. "They have no religion or morals, so their missile is an insult to the American way of life."

"What's the difference between a rocket and a missile?" I asked.

"That's your vocabulary homework for tonight," Mr. Herschberger said. "Find out."

Turns out a missile is always a weapon, and a rocket sometimes isn't.

Monday morning, Mr. Herschberger made an announcement. "Starting today, we are going to spend an extra fifteen minutes on math and science."

Lots of groans.

He held up his hand. "*Soviet* schools take those subjects seriously. Maybe that's why Sputnik succeeded." He opened a folder. "Russian pupils go to school *six* days a week, and have four hours of homework every night."

"Sign me up for the anti-Commie league," Sparky said. "I'll fight against *that* any day."

Everyone laughed, except Mr. Herschberger. "You think it's funny? By the time a Russian student finishes high school, he'll have two more *years* of education than you."

I looked down at my desk.

"I spent eighteen months in Korea fighting against Communism," Mr. H continued. "I disagree with everything it stands for. But Russian scientists created one of the greatest achievements in human history. And us? We're busy fighting our own citizens in Arkansas and Alabama." He closed the folder. "Foreign newspapers say that we're failing in the space race because we are a divided nation, that Americans hate each other more than we hate Communists. Are they right?"

"Heck no," Sticks said. "That's a load of bull—" He stopped before he said a playground word.

"Is it?" Mr. H held up a newspaper in another language, with a picture of a white woman screaming at a little black girl. "Looks like hate to me," he said. He laid down the paper just as the bell rang. "Think about that. I warn you, there are no easy answers."

I closed my book with a thump, harder than I meant to. I knew all this was important, but I liked easy answers, sometimes. Now it felt like *nothing* had one. Not school, not homework, not even baseball.

Chapter 17

Flying Dogs and Heroes

On October 26, the beeps stopped. Sputnik was still up there, but the signal's batteries had run out.

Two days later, there was a big brown envelope in the mail, postmarked Chattanooga. Jackie Mitchell wrote back to me! I'd almost given up hope, because it had been a couple of weeks, but I guess famous people must be pretty busy.

But there it was, and it was thick, like it was crammed *full* of stuff. I was so excited I jumped up and down for a whole minute before I opened it. Inside was an autographed picture and a newspaper clipping and a *three*-page letter in handwriting almost as messy as mine. I must have read it twenty times before dinner. By then it was starting to get kind of wrinkled.

"Mom, look." I showed her the picture and the letter when she got home. "Jackie Mitchell played for the House of David, too. For a couple of *years*." I pointed to the clipping. "I wonder if she knew Babe Didrikson?"

"Sounds like another trip to the library."

"Yeah." I smiled. "I might need some more folders."

Thursday was Halloween. Right after dinner, I met Jules at the mailbox on the corner to go trick-or-treating. I wore my baseball clothes, and stuck black letters that said MITCHELL to the back of my jersey. No one got it. I think most people thought I was a boy. "Oh, how cute! You're Mickey Mantle, aren't you?" At first, I tried to explain who Jackie Mitchell was. No one cared. After a block, I just nodded and took their candy.

A white lab coat and black plastic glasses turned Jules into a Russian scientist. She'd covered a basketball with tinfoil and glued painted straws to it, to look like Sputnik. A lot of people gave her funny looks, and one guy slammed his door on us. No treats there, but we did okay. Lots of little Mars bars. Space candy.

It had been a great week.

The weekend, not so much.

Jules's parents were going out Saturday night, and instead of getting a sitter, her mom let her come to my house for a sleepover. By then I wasn't really in the mood. From up in the attic, I heard her say hi to my mom, then skip up the stairs. She started talking before she even got through the door. "You shoulda seen my mom! All dressed up for this fancy-schmancy party, in high heels and—Why are you sitting in the dark?"

"Because."

"Can I turn on a light?"

"I guess."

Jules flipped the switch by the door. She dropped a marble into one of the chutes on the Wall and smiled when it hit three of the xylophone bars, one right after another, making a chime sound that lingered for a few seconds. "Pretty darn nifty," she said.

"Yeah."

"What's eating *you* today?"

"Nothing."

I was sitting on the floor all the way under the big old table that had been covered with my research for the last couple of weeks. Jules walked over and ran a hand over the empty surface. "Does this mean baseball's over for this year?"

I wiped my nose on my sleeve. "Baseball's over for*ever*."

"Why? Did you get another letter from Little League?"

"Worse."

"How?" Jules sat down on the floor in front of me.

I didn't say anything.

"Kates?"

I sighed. "I went to the library yesterday afternoon, and Miss Sherman had pulled out an old issue of a sports magazine for me. An article about a woman named Eleanor Engle."

"Another baseball player?"

"Uh-huh. She was signed to a minor-league team for the Athletics—five years ago, 1952."

"That's exactly what you've been looking for."

"I thought so, too. I was pretty excited. I used up another quarter for a crummy copy. There was a picture of her, in uniform, practicing with her team. Then I kept reading. She never played in a single game."

"Did she quit?"

"No!" I shouted that part. "The team manager canceled her contract, said he'd *never* let a girl play."

"That's terrible."

"It's even worse than that. This morning I went to the newspaper room on campus and read about a zillion articles about her, and they all said the same thing. The commissioner of *all* of baseball said that starting right that day, it was the *law* that no team was allowed to sign a woman as a player. *Ever*."

"So that's it?"

"Yep. Little League's still wrong about history, 'cause women did play, sometimes. But now? It really *is* a law. So—uncle."

"You're giving *up*?"

"Yeah. No." I pulled my legs up and wrapped my arms around my knees. "I don't know. What's the point?"

Jules sat there for a minute. “Because you like baseball. A lot.” She tilted her head and looked at me. “My piano teacher said she auditioned for the symphony, but they wouldn’t hire a woman. She kept playing anyway.”

“Did they change their minds?”

Jules scooted on her butt and scrunched in beside me. After a minute, she said, “Not for her, and it took a while, but yeah, eventually they did.” She leaned her head on my shoulder. “So will baseball.”

“Maybe.” I closed my eyes, and we sat like that until I heard the doorbell ring. A minute later Mom’s voice crackled through the intercom by the Wall. “Girls, pizza!”

“I’m not hungry,” I said.

“But I’m starving.” Jules crawled out and stood up. “C’mon.”

I shook my head.

“What am I gonna tell your mom?” She dusted off her pants. “How ’bout—you’ve turned into a troll and won’t come out from under your bridge?”

I shrugged.

“Fine. At least I don’t have to *lie* to her.” She stared at me for a minute, hands on her hips.

The intercom crackled again. My stomach rumbled. “I suppose I could eat,” I said.

So we did. Jules tried to get me in a better mood, telling knock-knock jokes and even busting out with a song, and it helped, some. We stayed up as late as Mom would let us, playing Clue and Sorry!, then slept in Sunday morning.

By the time we got dressed, it was after ten, and the sun was shining. Halfway down the stairs, I stopped, because the TV was on in the living room. That was weird. Mom didn't really like TV—even at night—except for *What's My Line?* and *I've Got a Secret.* Those shows had smart people on the panels, and she liked to guess along.

"What are you watching?" I asked.

"The news." She had her robe on, and even though she held a cup of coffee, she didn't look awake.

Jules frowned. "Why is there news *now*? It's Sunday morning, not six o'clock at night."

Mom put the cup down. "It's a special broadcast. The Russians launched another satellite."

"What's this one called?" I asked.

"Sputnik Two."

"Not much imagination."

"Maybe not, but it's definitely a scientific leap. This one has a passenger."

"The Russians put a *man* in space?" I sat down, hard, on the arm of the couch.

"No, a dog. Some sort of terrier, they said."

Jules shook her head. "Must be a *really* tiny one if it fits inside a basketball. We had a Scottie when I was little, and he was way bigger than that, even curled up."

"This satellite is much larger," Mom said. "It weighs almost as much as my car."

"Wow." I looked up at the ceiling, imagining a Nash Rambler speeding across the sky. "Where does the dog poop?"

Mom laughed. "They haven't mentioned that detail." She stood and stretched, then walked over and turned off the TV. "C'mon. I'll put the kitchen radio on and make us waffles."

That week, it was almost easy not to think about baseball. Current Events was all about the new satellite that the papers called Muttnik. They printed a lot of diagrams and technical details—this one was shaped like a cone, thirteen feet tall and six feet wide at the bottom. It weighed more than a thousand pounds and had radios and scientific transmitters in one section. But what the kids in my class wanted to talk about was the other section—the one with the dog.

We learned that she was a female, part terrier, part Samoyed. Sherm used the bad word for girl dog and had to sit through recess, even though he was correct. Her name was Laika, which meant "barker" in Russian. The scientists could listen to her heart and her breathing. She was chained up inside the capsule, was sometimes agitated, but was basically healthy. All week the papers were crammed full of dog facts, because Laika was more famous than Lassie or Rin Tin Tin. She was the most famous animal in history.

Every day there was a minute of silence on the radio. People were supposed to pray for Laika's safe return. Then, over the weekend, reporters found out that the Russians had never planned for Laika to come back, not alive. It was a one-way trip, and she'd only had enough oxygen for a week. She was going to die up there, was probably already dead. Nobody knew for sure, because Sputnik II had stopped sending signals: *its* batteries ran out after only seven days.

At Current Events that Monday, Janice couldn't stop crying and had to go see the nurse. All over the country, people protested, with signs and bullhorns and marches. Not because the Russians had beat us in space again, but because they had killed a poor little dog, which was really mean.

The Russians didn't do much for the rest of November. Neither did I. I shoved all my research into a drawer and slammed it, hard. Why bother? I felt like *my* batteries had run out. I watched a lot of TV and ate popcorn, read most of my sisters' old comic books, and dragged through my homework.

Then, the Monday after the long Thanksgiving weekend, Mr. Herschberger started class with an announcement instead of Current Events, and my life changed again.

He stood in front of his desk, his silver tie clasp glinting as he walked back and forth, gesturing with his hands. "For the last two months, we've read all about the Russians' accomplishments," he said. "Those scientific feats have made a lot of people nervous. They say we're behind in the 'space game.' We build cars with tail fins, bigger hi-fis, pink refrigerators and stoves to match, while *they* build missiles and satellites. They say Americans are soft."

He looked around the room, nodding, like he was giving a speech.

"Are *we* the society that killed a defenseless animal? No. That's not the American way. Communists don't believe in God—we do. They don't believe in free speech—we do. For all their scientific achievements—and they are impressive, make no mistake about that—the Russians are a *morally* bankrupt people."

He tapped one fist into his other hand. And we "Americans—we most certainly are not." He looked out into the class. "Are we?"

All around me I heard kids muttering. Nobody's hand went up. No one was sure what we were supposed to say. Finally Pinky said, "Nope."

"That's right," Mr. H said. "You're old enough to understand good citizenship, and to tackle schoolwork that goes beyond memorizing facts and dates. So I'm going to challenge you with a research project."

Lots of kids groaned. Even *harder* homework?

"I want each of you to choose an American hero. A person who made a difference, who demonstrated that freedom and courage and skill are at the heart of the *American* way of life."

Annie raised her hand. "Can it be anybody, or just people from history?"

"Current events or history," he said.

Then it seemed like everyone's hand was in the air with a question.

"Does it have to be someone famous?"

"Can I pick my dad?"

"Does it have to be a man, or do women count?"

Mr. Herschberger frowned, like he was thinking, then held up his hand. "Any American hero. Or heroes, I suppose, like the Little Rock Nine. People you admire, whose example you'd like to follow." He sat down on the edge of his desk. "I'm not going to give out assignments. I want you to take the initiative, develop independent thinking. Think of this as your chance to educate *me*."

Mike raised his hand. "If sports aren't allowed in Current Events, how 'bout for this?"

"No, Mike. I'm talking about more than—"

Shirley started talking as soon as her hand shot up. "What about Jackie Robinson? He played sports, but he be a hero for civil rights, too."

Mr. H was quiet for a minute. "I would accept that," he

said finally. He looked at Mike. "If you do choose a sports figure, I will hold you to a *very* high standard. A true hero does more than hit home runs. Understand?"

"Yeah," said Mike, without much enthusiasm.

"When's it due?" Andy looked worried. "We're visiting my grandma in Sacramento next weekend."

"You'll have plenty of time to do a thorough job," Mr. Herschberger said. "This is a *project*, not a paragraph. It's going to count for your *entire* Social Studies grade next marking period."

Behind me, I heard Pinky whistle, long and loud. "Jeez-sooey!" he said.

"That's right. Take it seriously, and give it plenty of thought. I want you to dig deep and investigate." He looked at the calendar on his desk. "Presentations will begin on the second Monday in February."

February? This was the beginning of December, so that was two whole months, more or less. Plenty of time. Minus the two weeks of Christmas vacation. Even Mr. H wouldn't expect us to work *then*.

Who did I want to—? And then I felt my whole body shiver. I thought of the folder filled with articles and pictures and letters. Whose example did I want to follow? Jackie Mitchell? Babe Didrikson? Eleanor Engle?

They were sports figures, though. Would any of them be enough for Mr. H's high standard? None of them had played for very long, and none of them had been able to change the law or anything, like Jackie Robinson. But he'd also said to choose people with skill and courage, and that was what I admired about them.

I felt my stomach unknot for the first time in weeks. Jules was right. I did love baseball. I wanted to find out if there were other girls like me. Mr. H had said to dig deep and investigate, and that was what I was going to do.

Chapter 18

Let's Make a Deal

As soon as the bell rang on Tuesday, I headed out the door toward the bike racks. It was cold but dry. I'd ridden to school that morning so I could get downtown to the library fast. The sun sets early in December, and Mom doesn't let me ride after dark. I was itching to get back to my research. Especially now that my social studies grade depended on it.

Then I saw Jules, standing by the wall, kicking rocks. Hard.

Jules wasn't a kicking kind of girl.

One rock clattered across the asphalt, ricocheting all the way to the monkey bars. I stopped a few feet away, not taking any chances. "Hey," I said. "What's up?"

"I hate school."

"No you don't."

"I hate fifth grade."

"Mrs. Lanagan?"

"She's not so bad." Jules shook her head. "It's that student teacher I told you about. Miss Kilgallen." She said the K so hard she just about spit. "She gave me a C-minus today."

"You're kidding."

"I wish." Jules kicked another rock. "She's teaching us biology, okay? Remember right before Thanksgiving, I told you we dissected peanuts, and observed them and took notes, then got to eat them?"

"Yeah. It sounded like fun."

"That part was. Except now we're drawing plants, and there's this stupid special lettering that you *have* to use to label the parts. The letters slant at this stupid angle, and they're supposed to be evenly spaced and all exactly the same stupid size." She made a face. "Mine were ordinary capital letters. She told me it was sloppy work."

"Handwriting." I blew a raspberry. "In high school, they'll make us type everything, so what's the big deal?"

"I don't know. But I've never gotten a C-minus in my whole life. My dad'll yell, and—" She kicked another rock. It bounced along the fence and disappeared into the grass.

Wham!

A white ball hit the chain-link with a rattling thud.

"Sorry," a voice yelled. "Didn't see you."

I turned my head, and Jules said a swear word I'd never heard her use before. She must have learned it at music camp. "That's her," she said, pointing. "*That's* Kilgallen."

I looked. A woman with short dark hair stood at home plate, in jeans and a thick gray sweatshirt, a bucket of balls behind her, a bat over one shoulder. I looked down the fence line and saw at least a dozen balls lying in the grass.

"Big deal. *Any*one can hit a softball," I said. Then I looked closer. *What the—?* It wasn't a softball, like the older girls used in gym. It was an actual regulation baseball. *Hmm.* That gave me an idea. I thought for a minute, then sighed inside my head, not out loud. The library would be open tomorrow. Jules needed a friend today. "Hey, Berg? Want some payback for that C-minus?" No way that teacher'd hit *my* pitching.

"Sure. What—?"

"C'mon." I tugged her arm. We walked across the grass until we were ten feet from home plate. The woman tossed another ball in the air. With a smooth swing, she knocked that one over the fence. "Need someone to toss a few to you?" I asked. I hoped she'd say yes. It had been more than a month since there'd been a game, and I missed the feel of my hand holding a ball. And I wanted to strike her out, for Jules.

The woman stopped her swing. "Hello, Juliana. Who's your friend?"

"Katy," Jules said. "Gordon. She has Mr. Herschberger."

"I see." She gave me a long look. "Can you throw?"

"The guys seem to think so," I said. "I'm a pitcher. *Over*hand."

"Are you now?" Miss Kilgallen leaned the bat against one hip. Close up I could see her arms had muscles. More than usual for a lady. "Okay. Why don't you show me what you've got. You need a glove?"

"Yeah. Mine's at home."

She stepped over to a duffel bag lying beside the bench and opened it. "Righty or lefty?"

"Righty."

I took off my coat and put it and my books on the bench. "Watch. This'll be fun," I whispered to Jules. I'd told her about my special pitch, but she was on the swings at recess and practiced piano after school, so she hadn't *seen* it yet.

I slid my hand into the leather glove, thumping the pocket, smiling at the feel of it as I walked out to the strip of rubber that marked the mound. Miss Kilgallen tossed me a ball, an easy, underhand lob.

She leaned the bat against the duffel. "I'll catch a couple, so you can warm up." She crouched behind the plate.

Hmm. She had a pretty good catcher's stance, like she'd done it before. I threw a couple of soft ones, feeling my arm loosen up, then hurled a fastball that made a good, satisfying *smack* when it hit her glove.

She flipped the ball back to me. "I'd say you're ready." She backhanded the glove into the duffel and picked up the bat. "Dazzle me."

I smiled. *Okay. You asked for it.* I went into my wind-up, leg high, and threw my second-best pitch, a slider that broke down and away, right above the corner of the plate. She swung and missed, and her eyes widened. She looked at me for a second, then tossed me another ball. That one had some zip on it.

I wound up again and threw the same pitch, to the other side of the plate. She missed again, not by much.

She smiled. "You got a Sunday pitch?"

"Matter of fact, I do." *This one's for Jules,* I thought. I turned the ball around in my glove until my fingers rested on the seams the way I wanted them and threw her the Gordon Special, the curving knuckleball that no one could hit. No kid, anyway.

It fluttered and floated to the plate, and she swung—hard—and missed, the ball hitting the backstop with a *thunk.* She almost lost her balance, then recovered and whistled through her teeth. "That's a nice pitch, kid."

"I know."

"Can you do it again?"

"Yep."

"Bring it on." She shouldered the bat again, her eyes narrowed, watching me.

She missed that one, too, but only by a whisker. My third try had too much spin, and she hit a solid line drive that cleared the outfield fence by at least a yard.

"That's a nice swing," I said after a minute. I was sweating under my wool jumper, and my breath was coming fast and hard, making little clouds in the cold air.

"It ought to be. I batted .315 last season." She tapped her bat against one shoe. ".268 lifetime."

Right, I thought. "Oh yeah? Where? No team's *allowed* to sign a woman."

"Three years at shortstop for the South Bend Blue Sox. When the league ended, I played two summers for Allington's All-Stars."

It was my turn to stare. "What league?" I started in toward home plate.

"The All-American Girls Baseball League."

"Really?!" I heard my voice squeak. "*Girls'* baseball?"

"The real McCoy."

There was a whole girls' baseball *league*? Zowie! "Will you tell me about it?" I asked. I heard my voice shake with excitement.

She looked at her watch. "I've only got time for the five-cent tour today."

"That's okay. Anything." I looked over at Jules. She rolled her eyes, but she was smiling. She nodded: go ahead.

"It started in 1943," Miss Kilgallen said. "Men were going off to war. Lots of people thought baseball would be canceled for the duration, so Mr. Wrigley, the guy who owned the Chicago Cubs, decided to start a league of women players. It was a publicity stunt, at first, to get crowds coming into the parks."

"So it *wasn't* real," I said. I kicked at the dirt.

"Hold on. It was plenty real for the gals playing. By the forties, the only organized games for women were softball leagues—don't get me started about softball—so the first couple of seasons they used underhand pitching and a bigger ball. By the end of the war, it was overhand pitching, with a big-league regulation ball, exactly like the guys." She looked at her watch. "Sorry. I've got a class tonight."

"Wait. Where can I find out more?"

"Lot of magazines did articles, including *LIFE*," she said. "Why so curious?"

I told her about Mr. H's assignment.

"Sounds like a good project." She patted me on the shoulder and zipped up her duffel.

"Hold on," Jules said. She gave me a wink. "How about a trade?"

Miss Kilgallen stopped in mid-zip. "For what?"

"Give me two weeks to practice my biology lettering. If I can get good enough for you to give me an A, you sit down with Katy and tell her the whole story."

Miss Kilgallen was quiet for a minute. "I do have a box of scrapbooks—programs and photos and line-up cards. And some addresses for the gals who swap Christmas cards with me. Would that help, Katy?"

"Would it! That would be—amazing." I could hardly believe it. I looked at Jules. "You'd do that for me?"

"Shazam," she said. "We gotta stick together, right? Besides, you've been a sad sack for a month. No fun at all." She held out her hand to Miss Kilgallen. "Deal?"

"No special favors. You'll have to really *earn* that A."

"I know," Jules said. "I take piano lessons. I'm used to practicing."

"Sounds like a win-win, then." She shook. "If you can ace lettering, I'll introduce your buddy to the best ball players she's never heard of." She threw the duffel over her shoulder and headed for the parking lot.

"Thanks, Jules." I put on my coat. "How'm I gonna pay you back?"

"I'll think of something. Besides, Daddy promised if I get all As this period—except for gym—I can get a new puppy."

"That'd be neat." I tucked my books under my arm. "If my handwriting wasn't even worse than yours, I could— Wait." I snapped my fingers. "Maybe I *can* help. Dewey had to take drafting and mechanical drawing, and I *know* there are lettering books up in the attic. They're all mine now."

"Super. With some diagrams and instructions, it *can't* be any harder than playing Bach."

That had to be true. I'd seen the sheet music. "Aces. I'll get my bike. Let's go check out my inheritance."

Chapter 19

Flopnik-land

We got Hostess CupCakes from the breadbox—my mom might not bake much, but she was pretty good at shopping—and went up to the attic. When Suze moved to the city, she'd taken a lot of her books, but Dewey was all the way across the country and had left most of hers behind. Shipping them was expensive, and MIT had a pretty good library.

Sure enough, we found a really old book—from 1917—called *Freehand Lettering for Engineers.* It had tiny print and even the pictures looked boring to me, but Jules flipped through the pages and smiled. "All right! That's the same as Kilgallen's."

"I guess for lettering, it doesn't matter what kind of scientist you are," I said.

"Probably not," Jules agreed. "This shows *exactly*

how to draw each letter and number, with the height and the spacing. Everything I need." She turned another page and let out a *whoop.* "Look. Your sister even left a bunch of practice sheets." She showed me some mimeographed pages, the purple ink a little faded, with identical rectangles full of dotted-line letters that reminded me of kindergarten alphabets.

"That'll help?"

"It's *perfect.* Can I take this home?"

"Sure. I think there may be even more lettering junk." I rooted around in Dewey's old desk and found a ruler, a wooden triangle, and a metal alphabet stencil. "Hey. You could just use this," I said, holding up the stencil. "All your letters will be the same, automatically."

"That feels like cheating." Jules frowned. "I'm not going to welch on a deal."

"Okay." I put the stencil back. "Take the rest, though. They'll keep your lines straight, once you've run out of practice sheets."

"Those'll be useful." Jules looked as happy as if I'd given her a box of toys. I started to kid her about being so weird she got excited about *homework,* then remembered that I'd been jumping up and down at the idea of spending the afternoon in the library, and shut up.

We went downstairs. "What's all that?" Mom asked.

Jules explained.

"Ah, inclined Gothic," Mom said. "I had to learn it, too,

back in the day. In fact—" She opened the book to the inside cover and pointed to a name in blue ink: *M. Weiss, 414 Schaefer Hall*. "This was mine, in college. I passed it on to Dewey." She handed it back to Jules. "Nice to know it's still serviceable."

"And how," Jules said, and tucked it into her binder.

◇ ◇ ◇

I rode my bike to school again Wednesday. I could hardly wait to get to the library. Now that I'd found out there'd been a girls' baseball league, I knew just what to look for.

Usually the last ten minutes of class we tidied up our desks and made sure we had all the homework handouts. I had my books piled up and ready when Mr. H rapped on his desk for attention.

"I have a special homework assignment for all of you tonight," he said. The usual groans from the usual boys. Mr. H just smiled. "I think you may enjoy this one. How many of you have seen Walt Disney on television?"

Almost everyone raised their hand.

"Good. Tonight's program is about space exploration. Watch it, take notes if you like, and be prepared to share your thoughts tomorrow morning."

"Wait, we get to watch *TV* for homework?" Pinky asked. "And it's not even the news?" He put a hand to his forehead, like he was going to faint with surprise.

Andy said, "You're okay, Mr. H."

"I have my moments. I might even—"

I usually listened to Mr. H, because he's kind of interesting. But today, the moment the bell rang, I was on my feet and out the door before he even finished his sentence. At the library, I spent almost two hours with the *Readers' Guide*, making lots of notes. In the 1940s, there were a bunch of articles about women and baseball. *LIFE*, *Time*, *Collier's*. I had a hard time believing Little League hadn't known about *any* of that. Their whole letter was starting to look like a big fat lie.

I'd just gotten to the year I was born, 1947, when the lights flickered. I put a tiny piece of paper in that volume, to mark my place, then reshelved it and headed for home.

Dinner was leftover chicken, tater tots, and fruit cocktail. Walt Disney didn't come on until 7:30, so I did my other homework in the kitchen while Mom marked up papers with a red pen.

After about fifteen minutes, she blew out a big sigh and threw the pen onto the table. "You know what? I need a break." She looked at the clock. Quarter after seven. "That program sounds interesting. I think I'll join you. Want some popcorn?"

Wow. Like I said, Mom almost never watched TV. I could only nod.

I went into the living room with my notebook and a

pen and turned the dial to channel 7—KGO. Mostly I liked Disney. It was different every Wednesday, sometimes cartoons, sometimes a western like *Davy Crockett*, depending on which part of Disneyland Tinker Bell decided to visit—Fantasyland or Adventureland. I guessed tonight would be Tomorrowland, since the program was about space, and we weren't actually *there* yet.

The show was called *Mars and Beyond*. It was pretty interesting. The first part was history, with cartoons, so it wasn't too boring, then a nifty science-fiction part, with spaceships and goofy-looking martians. Real people, scientists in white shirts and bow ties, showed pictures of other scientists and telescopes. More cartoons about what life on Mars *might* look like, then serious-looking men talking about rockets and orbits and the future.

The next morning, Current Events was all about space. Not just Disney space, either. The news was full of real rockets. Tomorrow, at a place called Cape Canaveral, the United States was finally going to beat Russia in the "space race." We were going to launch our *own* satellite, Vanguard TV3. Personally, I thought our scientists could have tried a little harder to come up with a catchy name—they were competing against *Sputnik*, right? Mr. H was excited anyway.

Our country wasn't keeping it a secret. Not like the

Communists. The launch was going to be on TV—*live* TV—all over the country, he told us.

"I'd assign it for homework," he said, "but the launch is scheduled for 11:45 tomorrow morning, in Florida. Unfortunately, that's *eight* forty-five here in Berkeley, and as you know the bell rings at the stroke of nine. We'll have to settle for listening to the commentary on the radio."

My mom had a different idea. "I'll write you a late note. Your dad called me at work this afternoon, and I promised I'd let you stay home to watch."

"Is Vanguard one of *his* rockets?"

"No, it's a navy project, and he's working with the army. Still, every scientist in the country has their fingers crossed for this one."

The next morning at 8:30, I sat on the couch watching TV with my mom, for the second time in two days. I wore my school clothes, my books stacked on the coffee table. So far, all we'd seen were CBS News guys sitting at a desk, talking and talking, then cutting away to pictures of the satellite and to the rocket sitting on the launchpad. From the pictures, our satellite looked a lot like Sputnik—a round ball with *six* antennas sticking out of it. It was tiny, though, only three pounds—the size of a softball, not a basketball.

The rocket was as tall as a seven-story building. The

ones in comic books had fins and portholes, but ours just looked like a giant black-and-white pencil pointing straight up.

At 8:45, the picture on the TV switched over to the launchpad, and a man started counting down from ten. When he got to zero, I saw gray smoke come out of the bottom of the rocket. It went up in the air for about two seconds with a loud crackling sound, and then it started to sink again, like it was going backwards, drilling *into* the ground.

Then it exploded. Smoke and flames went out in every direction, and in the center of all of that, the rocket just fell over sideways. That was the last we saw of it, because now the whole TV screen was filled with a gigantic fireball, except in black and white. It got bigger and bigger until it looked a lot like the pictures of the atomic bomb. The cameras kept running for a few seconds, then the screen went back to the news guys, who looked as shocked as everyone else, but were trying to sound calm and professional.

Mom turned the set off and lit a cigarette.

"*That* didn't go well," she said. She looked at the clock. Twelve minutes to nine. "Here's your note," she said. "If you hustle, you might even make it before the bell rings."

I did. Mr. H had the radio on his desk. The news guys were calling our *own* rocket Flopnik and Oopsnik.

Everyone in my class looked stunned, like the world had ended. Maybe it had.

In the world series of space, the Russians were up, two to nothing, and the home team—America—had just struck out.

Chapter 20

Strawberries and the Lipstick League

The last day of school before Christmas vacation, the lunchroom was buzzing with kids making plans for two weeks of freedom.

"I did it!" Jules plopped down next to me in the cafeteria and carefully laid a piece of paper a few inches from my tray.

It was a pencil drawing of a daisy with lines coming out from various parts, connecting to words I'd never heard of: *bracts, stamen, stigma.* The words looked so neat they could have been printed by a machine. At the top of the page, in bright red ink, was a big capital A in a circle, and a handwritten note: *Bravo!*

"You got an A in handwriting." I was impressed.

"Yep." She grinned. "Kilgallen even shook my hand. She's student-teaching gym at another school after New

Year's, so she said you should talk to her right after the bell, if you still want to know about baseball stuff."

"You bet'cha." For the last two weeks, while Jules had practiced—letters *and* piano—I'd been in the downtown library most afternoons. I'd finally gotten to this year in the *Readers' Guides*, and had read articles in every old magazine that library had. The campus one had others, but I needed Mom for that, and she'd been too busy with final exams.

"I got a new game for Hanukkah," Jules said. "It's called Why, and it's like Clue, except with detectives. Want me to bring it over tomorrow?"

"Sure." We almost never played at her house. Her mom was really strict, and we couldn't make noise or be messy. Their house was so clean there were plastic covers on the dining room chairs. "We're going to my gramma's tonight. For latkes and stuff."

"Us too. Yum." Jules picked up the paper by its corners so it didn't accidentally get into my sloppy joes. "See ya."

Mr. H gave us a pep talk about keeping up with our projects and current events over the holidays. Nobody paid much attention. When the bell rang, I said "Merry Christmas" to him, then headed for the other fifth-grade room.

Miss Kilgallen was packing up her books and papers, and looked pretty busy. She gave me her address and phone number and said I could come over to her apartment Monday afternoon.

I was *almost* glad it was rainy and there weren't any games at the lot, because that meant I had more time to do interviews and other research. It was getting pretty interesting, and I was even finding out a bunch of other cool stuff that had nothing to do with baseball.

In the car on the way to Gramma's, I told Mom about some of it. "Did you know that women weren't even allowed to *vote* until 1920?"

She laughed. "I seem to remember that. I was your age when it happened. Did it come up in Current Events?"

"No, from my research." I told her more about the girls' baseball league and about Miss Kilgallen. She looked at me funny, because I was excited about doing homework on vacation, but it was a nice kind of funny.

Gramma let me light the four candles on the menorah while she said the prayers. I touched the shamas candle to the pale white wicks and watched as they bloomed into blue and yellow flames. Mom did the dishes after dinner while the old ladies and I played dreidel. I won a bunch of chocolate money. Gramma handed me a wrapped present, and asked if I was too old for dolls now. I made a face. When I opened it, she laughed. It was a Mr. Potato Head. "Because you like my latkes so much."

Jules wasn't as happy on Saturday. *Her* grandmother had given her a dress to wear at her next piano recital.

"You *do* have to look fancy for those, right?" I asked.

"Yeah, but—" She frowned. "See the label?" She showed me the tag at the back of the neck: CHUBETTES.

"That's rude." Jules wasn't exactly skinny, but really, a dress from the Fat Department? What a lousy present. We played her new game, twice, then went to the Elmwood soda fountain to drown her sorrows.

After lunch Monday I gathered up my baseball notebook, a pencil, two pens, and my Kodak Brownie camera.

"Do you want one of my handbags for all that?" Mom asked.

"A *purse*? No."

She sighed. "You and your sister. Some anthropologists think that the first human tool might have been a carrying sack, not a hammer. A hunter-gatherer society needs—"

She saw the look on my face.

"Sorry. I think Suze left an army surplus thing in the hall closet."

I found a green canvas bag with a leather carrying strap. It looked *nothing* like a purse. All my supplies fit inside, and I felt like a reporter, or a private eye on an investigation. I slung it over my shoulder.

Miss Kilgallen lived in an apartment on Euclid Avenue. She answered my knock wearing blue jeans and a gray Cal sweatshirt. Her place was one big room with a tiny kitchen at one end. A cardboard box lay on the couch, next to the kitchen table, a big black scrapbook in the center.

"I have apple juice and some cookies," she said. "Store-bought, I'm afraid."

"Sure, ma'am. Thanks."

She smiled. "I'm not a teacher right now. You can call me Deb."

"Okay." I put down my bag while she got the snacks.

"So," she said. "You have questions for me?"

I opened my notebook. "To start with, how many teams were there in the All-American Girls Baseball League? Some articles said four, some said a lot more."

"Four, the first season. That was 1943. The Racine Belles, the South Bend Blue Sox, the Kenosha Comets, and the Rockford Peaches."

"Where are *those* towns?"

"Wisconsin, Indiana, and Illinois. All near Chicago."

"Because of the Cubs."

"Got it in one. The league expanded into Michigan and had ten teams by '48. I started in '53. By then it was back down to six."

"Were all the players from Chicago?"

"In the beginning, there were a lot of local girls." She twisted an Oreo apart and licked off the cream part. "But scouts went all over the country, looking at softball leagues, some factory teams, even some former Bloomer Girls."

"What's a Bloomer Girl?" I asked.

"A whole 'nother story. Write it down and remind me. If we have time, I'll come back to it."

I did.

"Anyway, that first year, more than two hundred girls went to Chicago to try out for a spot on one of the teams. Scouts looked for baseball talent, but turned down a lot of girls because they weren't—well, pretty—enough."

"What does that have to do with *base*ball?"

"Not a thing, but it was part of the deal. Wrigley wanted players who looked like ladies and played like men."

"That explains some of the articles I found at the library." I turned a page in my notebook. "'Beauty at the Bat,' 'The World's Prettiest Ballplayers.'"

"I have that one." She opened the scrapbook. "The last line's a corker: 'It's Valentine's Day all season in the Lipstick League.'"

We both rolled our eyes.

"I've seen a couple of pictures. Did you really have to wear *dresses* for uniforms?"

"Yep." She turned a few pages back and pointed to a program.

On the cover was a woman leaping up, her glove held high in the air. She wasn't ugly, but I didn't think she was any Miss America, either. She wore a cap and baseball shoes and high socks, and a dress with a belt and big buttons up the left side. It was pretty short, way above her knees, so it wouldn't get in the way much. But it was still a dress.

"I know. The fans wanted to see ladies, not tomboys. Or so the bigwigs thought. We had very strict rules: no smoking or drinking, no slacks in public."

I made a raspberry and sat back in my chair. "I thought you said you played *real* baseball." I felt—I don't know. Cheated. Disappointed.

"Oh, we did, Katy." Deb smiled. "The brass—all men, of course—made those rules, but *we* were playing hardball. Let me show you something I bet you *haven't* seen." She rummaged in a box. "Gotcha," she said, and put a book down on the table, a paperback, about the size of a *Reader's Digest*. "The Major League Baseball yearbook from 1947," she said. "See who's on the front cover?"

"Stan Musial. 'Player of the Year.' So?"

"So turn it over to the *back* cover."

I did, and my mouth dropped open. It was a woman, swinging a bat, hard. "Sophie Kurys," I read. "'Player of the Year.'" At the bottom, in a green box, it said ALL-AMERICAN GIRLS BASEBALL LEAGUE.

I took a picture of it with my camera.

"Look inside."

The book was full of major-league stats and box scores. The last twenty pages were all about the girls' league—photos, articles, lists of RBIs, ERAs, batting champs, playoffs.

"Real enough for you?"

I nodded, too busy writing to talk. "This Sophie Kurys, she had 201 stolen bases in *one* season?"

Deb laughed. "Out of 203 attempts. She stole more than a thousand, lifetime."

My eyes went wide. "Ty Cobb only had 892. That's the record."

"For men, maybe." She took a drink of her juice. "And Cobb did it wearing pants. Sophie slid in on bare legs."

"Ouch." I'd bunged up my arms enough times to know how much that hurt.

"I'll say. We wore shorts under our skirts, but some slides took the skin off from hip to knee. We called those 'strawberries'—in polite company."

I whistled and wrote down more names. Dorothy Kamenshek, 129 hits; Connie Wisniewski, a .81 ERA.

"That only covers the first four years," Deb said. She turned pages in the scrapbook. "Dottie Schroeder played all twelve seasons. The manager of the Cubs told her if she was a man, he'd sign her for fifty thousand dollars." She ate a cookie, flipped pages. "We had more than a million fans in the best years. There were junior girls' teams all over the Midwest. But they petered out when the league died."

"I wish those were still around."

"Me too. That's the biggest hurdle, for players like us. Boys are coached and taught the fundamentals at every level—Little League through college. Without those opportunities, girls will never have the skills and experience to compete."

"Then people will say we can't play."

She shook her head. "Anyone who says girls can't play baseball is just ignorant about the history of the game. More than six hundred girls played in my league alone."

I sputtered and almost spit apple juice all over the table. "So how come *everyone* doesn't know about that? How come it's not in books with all the other baseball history?"

"That is a very, very good question."

I sighed. "And there are no easy answers?"

"Well, I suppose since the teams were all in the Chicago area, there wasn't as much coverage nationally. Just a handful of articles. Plenty of press locally, though. Look." She turned page after page in her scrapbook, dozens of yellowing newspaper clippings. "It seems impossible that it only ended three years ago."

"What *happened*?" I asked, louder than I meant to.

"The crowds stopped coming. People who wanted to watch baseball turned on the TV. I was lucky. I played on a traveling team for a few more summers. Even that went belly up last August."

"Will there be another league?"

"Who knows? No reason we should stop. Women have been playing baseball since the game started."

She turned another page. "Here's a good example."

I leaned over to look closer. "Lois Youngen," I said. "What's she famous for?"

"Nothing, really. But when we were teammates, she told stories about a woman from her hometown, a pitcher named Alta Weiss. *She* started playing in 1907, formed her own team, the Weiss All-Stars. Her father even built her a field."

"1907? Too bad I can't travel back in time. Then I could talk to her."

"You can, if you want. She's retired now—went to medical school on the money she earned from baseball—lives in that same little town in Ohio. Lois will have her address."

"Really? She's alive?"

"And kicking. In her late sixties now, I think."

"Was she a watcha-callit?" I looked at my notes. "A Bloomer Girl?"

"Nope. They played around the same time, though." Deb put down her glass. "You know who *was* a Bloomer Girl? Miss Lowry, the gym teacher at the junior high."

I shivered.

"What's wrong?"

"My friend's sister has her. They call her the Dragon Lady."

She laughed. "As far as I know, she doesn't breathe fire. But she is tough. She played professional ball for close to twenty years. Talk to her and you'll get some great stories."

"That might be worth it," I said, trying to sound brave.

Deb showed me dozens of articles and newspaper clippings. I filled my notebook with dates and names and addresses until the sun started to drop behind the buildings.

"I should send you home before it gets too dark," she said, looking out the window at the red-gold light.

"Probably." Had it really been four *hours*? "Can I ask you something first?"

"Shoot."

"If so many women have played baseball over the years, how can Little League get away with telling everyone it's always been a man's sport?"

"That's mostly what we're taught in college, too, in the P.E. program. Baseball is for boys, softball is for girls. End of story." She drained the last of her juice. "Doesn't seem to matter that it contradicts actual history. It's a myth that they've told thousands of boys every year. Sooner or later, *everyone* starts believing it's true."

"Except us."

She smiled. "Except us." She ran a finger along the edge of a ticket stub, a sad smile on her face. "Best years of my life," she said softly. "We were just ballplayers, doing what we loved to do best. We had no idea how special it really was."

Chapter 21

A New Kid in Town

School started up again the first Monday in January. 1958. That felt so weird. I kept forgetting and writing 1957 instead.

When I walked into room 120, I wasn't sure I was in the right *place*, either. There were twenty-nine kids in my class, and we each had a desk. Now, instead of six rows all lined up facing the blackboard, they had been rearranged into five clusters, three desks on a side, facing across at each other.

Everyone stood around the room, talking. I went over to PeeWee.

"Where are we supposed to sit?" I asked. I'd left books and papers inside my desk before vacation. With the lids all closed, I had no idea which one was mine.

"I dunno," he said. "I guess we'll—"

Mr. Herschberger clapped his hands. "Good morning! Happy New Year!" He had on a bright-red tie. "As you can see, with the new year comes a new way of learning." He smiled. "Shake things up a bit, get a fresh perspective."

He pointed to the cluster of desks next to the playground door. "This is table one. That'll be—" He looked at his clipboard. "—Anderson, Bernstein, Yakimora, Morton, Dickinson, and Chen."

The six kids whose names he'd called stepped away from the wall and walked over to their desks. Joyce Chen lifted one lid, and then Mr. Herschberger said, "Your names are written on a piece of tape on your desktop. Everything *inside* is exactly as you left it—with the exception of Mr. Bernstein's sandwich, which has gone to the great cafeteria in the sky." He held his nose. "Got a little stinky there, Mike."

Mike's face turned red, and he ducked his head and sat down.

"Table two," Mr. Herschberger said, pointing. He read off the next six names. I was at table five, which was next to the cloakroom, with Pinky, Andy, Whiz, Madge, and a Negro boy I'd never seen before. The tape on his desk said BELL.

I sat down and opened the lid. For a minute, I looked through my papers and junk, so I wasn't staring too hard at the new kid.

"I'm Chip," he said finally. "We moved here from Oakland a couple of weeks ago."

When everyone had sat down and Mr. Herschberger checked all the names off his attendance list—Janice and Mark were out sick—he pointed to our table. "You've probably noticed that we have a new student. Will you introduce yourself?"

He stood, his face in an embarrassed grin. "I'm Chip Bell," he said, and sat down again.

I watched Mr. Herschberger look down at his clipboard and raise his eyebrows, then nod and make a note. I figured Chip was a nickname, like I was Katy, not Kathleen. I snuck a peek at him and wondered what the long version of Chip was. Then Mr. H cleared his throat and said, "Now, who wants to start Current Events for 1958? Patty? Good."

Kids from other tables reported on the news, which was mostly about how Sputnik—the first one—had stopped orbiting the earth and had burned to a crisp in the atmosphere before it could crash. Chip sat right across from me, so I couldn't help looking at him all morning. He was a little taller than me, with a fuzz of very short black hair, long arms, and long, skinny fingers. He was quiet, but smart. He breezed through the first math quiz of the year.

At lunch, I found out he was also a slugger.

We'd had morning recess in the gym, and they were

showing cartoons in the auditorium so nobody *had* to go outside. The weather was pretty chilly, but it hadn't rained for the last couple of days. A bunch of us were itching to play some ball, so we took our sandwiches out to the field. There was another new kid, Freddy, from Mrs. Lanagan's class. We had almost enough for a real game.

Chip looked surprised—okay, shocked—when he saw me walk up. He didn't say anything, which was also smart. He was new, and needed to watch how this pack of boys ran things.

Four guys flipped coins, and PeeWee and Matt got to choose sides. Chip's eyes got really wide when PeeWee picked me first. I could almost see his brain working: *They let a girl play? They* want *her to play?*

Freddy got picked fourth, by Matt. *He* didn't stay quiet. "Hey, hey. This is gonna be a *cinch*," he said, in a loud, boasty voice. "Their team has to play with a *girl*." He turned to the other guys, waiting for them to jump in and agree, but they didn't.

"Maybe," Sherm said. He smiled, that way boys do when they're about to pull off a good prank.

Chip was on Matt's team, too. He whispered something, and Matt nodded. Chip trotted over to the rock that was first base.

The first three batters on my team went out one-two-three—pop-up, grounder, an out at first. Chip was *fast*.

I took the mound. Freddy, the new boy, was up first.

I could see why. He was a meaty kid who looked like he could connect. He stood with the bat on his shoulder and gave me a mean sort of smile. "C'mon, sister. Lemme see your very best powder-puff stuff."

"Aw, for the love of Pete. Shut your trap." PeeWee got into his crouch. Freddy looked back, surprised. PeeWee gave me the sign—fastball. I shook him off. Another sign—slider. I nodded, curled my hand around the ball, and threw.

Freddy swung and missed. "Lucky pitch," he said.

I looked around at the other guys. Nobody was smiling at Freddy. I wound up, threw him another slider.

Swing and a miss.

Freddy's big face was red now, but his knuckles were white around the bat. He glared at me like he had Superman's heat vision and could burn a hole right through my face.

I held up my fist, closed, and behind Freddy, PeeWee nodded. I fingered the seams and threw a sweet knuckleball. It bobbed and floated and was nowhere near Freddy's bat when he swung, going all the way around.

"Strike three," PeeWee said. "Next?"

Freddy stomped back to the end of the line and didn't say another word.

I missed with my next pitch, and Matt hit a long, high ball out into left, but Whiz ran fast and got underneath it in time. Two outs.

Chip came up to the plate. He took my first strike looking, his bat never leaving his shoulder, and I saw him nod to himself. He took a big cut at the next one, just missing it, and shook his head. On the next pitch—a good slider, too—he waited half a fraction of a second, then slammed the ball all the way out of the playground, over the chain-link fence and into a clump of bushes in a neighbor's yard.

I watched him circle the bases. When he rounded third, he grinned. After a minute, I grinned back, and after another, the first bell rang, and we scrambled to gather up all the gear and get back to class.

We only got to play once more before it rained for three days, heavy enough to keep us inside and make the field a muddy swamp. It was just starting to dry up again by the end of Chip's second week. He was waiting outside the door when I came out with my coat and my lunch box on Thursday.

"You doin' anything this weekend?" he asked.

"Not much. Why?"

"Wanna, you know—?" He swung his math book like it was a bat, his voice sounding like it was no big deal.

"Sure," I said, like it wasn't a biggie to me, either. But inside I felt like I'd gotten a little shock, like walking across carpet and touching a doorknob. Getting an invite to play with guys I *hadn't* known since first grade? Wow. "When's the game?"

"Saturday afternoon. There's a dirt lot on my block." He dropped his math book to his side. "My cousin Josh usually pitches, except he cut up his finger trying to whittle with his new knife."

"Messes with your grip," I agreed. "Where do you live?"

"On Colby, a block up from Alcatraz."

"Okay." I looked down at my skirt. "Are they gonna make a stink about me being—?" I let the obvious hang there. "I mean, I play in jeans and a jersey, and you can call me Gordon. Maybe no one'll notice right off."

He thought for a minute. "Ricky might pitch a fit, only until he tries to hit your slider." He smiled. "Won't matter, though. It's my bat, so I get to pick sides." He looked at me. "My guys—they all colored. That gonna bother *you*?"

"Can they play?"

"Yeah. Some more'n others."

"Then I'm jake."

"Solid," he said. "Come by 'round noon."

Chapter 22

Bloomer Girls

I thought a little about Chip on my way home, but mostly about Miss Lowry. All the schools were closed over vacation, and since then I'd been working up the courage to pick up the phone to call her. I wasn't exactly *scared*, but talking to the Dragon Lady? Everyone's older sister had a story about *her*.

I ate a lunch box bag of Fritos before I picked up the kitchen phone and called Willard Junior High. The girl who answered said, "Hold on a minute," and the next thing I knew, a woman who sounded like she had a bad cold said, "Hello. This is Miss Lowry. What can I do for you?"

Dragon-like voice, but as polite as one of Mom's club ladies.

"Hi," I said, holding the receiver so tight my hand hurt.

"My name is Katy Gordon, and I'm in the fifth grade at LeConte, and I'd like to make an appointment to interview you." I stopped to breathe. "Please?"

I heard a chuckle on the other end of the line. "*Interview* me? About what?"

"Baseball."

"Baseball."

Silence. Five seconds. Then ten. I couldn't stand it any longer. "Miss Kilgallen said you'd have interesting stories."

"Miss—oh, *Deborah.*" The gruff voice sounded surprised, but happy. "I suppose I do, at that. Tell you what. Volleyball practice ends in fifteen minutes. Can you be here by then?"

"Today?" I heard my voice squeak.

"I'll be here for another hour or so, and the team has an away game tomorrow."

"Today—today is fine." My hands felt sticky with sweat.

"Good. Come to the side door. It's marked GYMNASIUM. I'll let you in."

I grabbed my notebook and Suze's army bag with my interview gear and quick-walked the three blocks to the junior high. A dozen older girls streamed out the gym door, chattering and paying no attention to me.

"Katy, is it?" asked the voice from the phone.

Standing in the doorway was a wrinkle-faced woman, a bit shorter than me, her yellow-gray hair pulled back into a bun that glittered with gramma-like hairpins. Her arms and legs were skinny and tan under a pair of blue shorts and a white shirt with WJHS across the front. A silver whistle on a braided leather lanyard hung around her neck.

"Yes, ma'am," I said. "Miss Lowry?" I thought for a second, and held out my hand.

She shook it, stronger than she looked. "Come in. We can talk in my office." I followed her across the polished gym floor and into a locker room, damp with steam from afternoon showers, towels draped over wooden benches. The tiled walls and floor echoed as we walked, even though we were both wearing sneakers.

Her office was smaller than our upstairs bathroom. One wall held shelves of trophies and ribbons and framed photos of rows of girls holding basketballs or field hockey sticks or crossed bats. Some of them wore shorts and shirts; others had sailor blouses and weird puffy pants from a long time ago.

Miss Lowry sat down behind a beat-up wooden desk and pointed at a straight-back chair. "Sit, please." She opened a plaid thermos bottle and poured steaming liquid into the cup-lid. "I'd offer you coffee, but it might stunt your growth." She looked at me and smiled. "So, baseball," she said, taking a sip. "How come?"

She looked straight at me, her blue eyes sharp. I was glad I wasn't in her office for a lecture—or detention.

"Deb said you used to play. Professionally."

"A long, long time ago. Why the curiosity now?"

The story came easily. I had it down to a few sentences that covered all the essential facts. Little League, at first, then my American heroes assignment, how I was looking for women who had played *real* baseball, who had tried to change things.

When I took a breath, she smiled. "When they shut you out, you didn't roll over and take no for an answer, eh? That took some spunk."

I shrugged. "They're wrong." I opened my notebook. "When did *you* start playing?"

She put her cup down. "As soon as I could walk, I suppose. I came from a big family—five boys and three girls. There was always *some* game going on in the yard. My sisters sewed and cooked like good farm girls, but I was fielding grounders as soon as my chores were done. On summer weekends, barnstormers would come through Springfield—" She paused. "Do you know what those are?"

"Uh-uh."

"Teams that went from town to town. They had no stadium, no leagues, and not much organization, just traveled all season, challenging the locals, playing for part of the gate. As I remember, it cost a nickel to get a seat, another nickel for a sarsaparilla or a beer."

"And the men let you play?"

"Not a chance." She shook her head. "I just watched every game I could—from inside *and* outside the fence." She chuckled. "The summer I was fourteen—that was 1911—the Western Bloomer Girls came through. Maud Nelson ran that team." She looked at me. "Write *her* name down. She was a star pitcher, a manager, a team owner. She arranged all the promotion and publicity *and* supervised the scouting."

I wrote as fast as I could.

"My brothers and I ran down to the train station to watch them come in." She took another sip of coffee and looked over my head. Not *at* anything, but like she was watching a movie far behind me. "Maud Nelson knew how to put on a show. That's what sold tickets. She'd hired the local band to *oomp-pah-pah* down State Street, trumpets winking in the sun, a whole parade of ballplayers behind them, all in uniform—and all girls."

"Really?"

"Large as life. They wore pin-striped knickers and high socks, matching tunics and caps with WBG across the front. They marched down that street, laughing and waving to the crowd."

"Why were they called 'Bloomer Girls'? Did they always wear flowers?"

"Good guess, but no. Bloomers were loose pants, tight at the ankles—like Aladdin's. Named after Amelia Bloomer—early women's rights. The first outfits that allowed female athletes to actually *move* freely—ride a bike, hit a tennis ball, swing a golf club." She turned and pointed to one of the old pictures. "Those are bloomers. Maud's girls wore baseball pants, but the name had stuck."

"Oh." I wrote that down, too. I wasn't sure how much information I was going to need for my report, but I figured it was better to know too much than not enough. There *had* been a lot of girls like me, and I felt like we were sort of teammates. I wanted to find out everything I could about our stories, our history.

"Anyway," Miss Lowry continued, "we followed the parade to the ball park, and I spent my lunch money on one of the best games I'd ever seen. Afterward, I snuck through the bleachers to talk to their star pitcher. She had a whole crowd of people around her, but I finally got close enough that she noticed me—and my glove."

I was on the edge of my seat, listening.

"She smiled at me. 'Trying out for the team?' And I said, 'Can I?' She gave a little shrug and said, 'I'll give you a look-see.' I tell you, I was so nervous I couldn't say a word. But once I put my glove on and she tossed me a ball, I knew *exactly* what I was doing."

"I know *that* feeling," I said. My arms went all goose bumps, talking to a grown-up who *understood*.

"It's a great one, isn't it? I hit a few and took grounders at first—I was little and quick and not much got by me.

Maud Nelson herself came over to watch. 'You have a good arm,' Maud said. 'How old are you?' "

Miss Lowry drank the last of her coffee. "I almost lied, but that didn't seem right, so I told her, fourteen. She gave me a pat on the arm and said, 'Keep it up. If you still want to play in two years, write to me.' She handed me a real business card, with an address in Chicago."

"Did you?"

"You bet. I built up the muscles in my shoulders and arms doing chores—toting baskets of apples to the farm stand, pitching hay to the horses—and played ball every chance I got. I painted a bull's-eye on the side of an old shed and got to where I could hit it from anywhere in the yard. My brothers called me Bitty—bitty li'l thing. But I was faster than any of them."

"Then what?"

"When I turned sixteen, I wrote to her, and she sent a telegram for me to come down to Chicago on the train for a real tryout. My knees shook the whole way, but on the field I was fine. Maud signed me, right then and there, fitted me out with a flannel uniform. My mother had to take it in and hem it. She wasn't thrilled with the idea, but times were tough, and I promised I'd send money back home."

"You got paid?"

"Yes-siree Bob. Fifteen dollars a week. My brother Walt was a store clerk, and that was three dollars more than him. I played backup on first all that summer and saved as much as I could. I graduated high school, and put myself through college in the off-season. By the time I hung up my glove, I had a master's degree in physical education." She looked around her little office. "I started teaching here in 1929."

I did the math in my head. "So you played baseball—for money—for *sixteen* years?"

"Close to it. I played four years with the Western Bloomer Girls, then four with the All-Star Ranger Girls. Maud Nelson ran both teams."

I wrote all that down, then frowned. "That's only eight seasons."

She smiled. "You're good at numbers, too, huh? I finished up with the New York Bloomer Girls, Margaret Nabel's squad. She was a manager, not a player."

"How many Bloomer teams *were* there?"

"Too many to count, and not much ever written down about most of them. Dozens of teams, hundreds of girls, starting in the 1880s right through the 1930s—barnstormers, factory teams, locals—traveling all over the country, playing a different men's team at every whistle stop. I played in twenty-four states. It was a great education."

"Wow. Did you play with anyone famous?"

"Let me see. Most gals were only around for a season or two, then got married, and that was that. Hmm—" She drummed her fingers on her desk. "Edith Houghton." She spelled it. "She was a catcher for almost twenty years, then became a scout for the Phillies. First *female* scout in the majors." She smiled. "Oh, well—and I *did* tag out Rogers Hornsby once."

"What?" I almost dropped my pen. He was *really* famous, almost as famous as Babe Ruth, in the Baseball Hall of Fame and everything. "Did you play against the Cardinals or the Cubs?"

"Neither. Believe it or not, Hornsby was a Boston Bloomer Girl when he was in high school. He was what we called a 'topper'—played second base wearing bloomers and a girl's wig." She laughed. "That's *not* the picture you'll see on his baseball card."

"I'll say." I bit the top of my pen. "Isn't having a boy kind of—cheating?"

"Only if the team lied about it. A lot of the barnstorming teams were mixed. All that mattered was that you loved to play ball, and did it well enough to satisfy the crowds."

"So what happened to all those teams?"

"They came and went. The last ones died out in the thirties. It was the Depression, no one had a spare nickel to take in a ball game, and the teams didn't have the money to travel. And by then, girls were only being taught softball in school. What they called 'girls' baseball.'" She snorted. "We called it 'kitten ball' and 'pumpkin ball.' I'm not saying it's a bad game, but it sure isn't baseball. Nowadays, the curriculum is very clear: softball is for girls, baseball for boys. It's segregation, if you ask me. Separate but equal."

"Didn't the Supreme Court say that was illegal?"

"Not for sports." She sighed. "Does my heart good to see girls like you, wanting to play the real thing." She looked up at the clock on her wall. "Any more questions? I've got a hungry pup at home who thinks it's past his supper time."

"Oh, sorry," I said. I closed my notebook and stood up. "Thanks for telling me all this."

"My pleasure. I've got a scrapbook up in my attic. I'll bring it in and ask my assistant to make photocopies of some of the articles. Call me next week." She reached for her coat.

We went back through the empty locker room, my bag heavy on my shoulder. I was discovering amazing new facts, but they kept leading to the same conclusion: girls' baseball had a whole lot of history, but not a lot of *now*.

Chapter 23

Send in the Clowns

Saturday morning was crisp and clear, cool enough to need a jacket on the bike ride over to Chip's. I tossed my glove and an extra ball into the basket of my bike and rode down Russell to Regent, cutting over to Colby. These houses were smaller than the ones on my street. One of the driveways had two rusty, junked-up cars.

A knot of Negro boys stood on the sidewalk in front of a vacant lot, laughing and pushing at each other, trading insults. I pulled up and they all went quiet. Like me, they wore jeans with plaid flannel shirts and T-shirts underneath, and all had caps—Red Sox, Yankees, and a couple I didn't know: Monarchs and Creoles and Clowns. Minor leagues, I figured.

"Hey, Chip," I called.

He waved. "Gordon. Good." He turned back to his friends. "Boys, Gordon's in my class at school. Gonna pitch for my team today."

"We gotta play with some *white* kid?" one of the others said, making a face like he had to eat liver.

"Baseball's integrated now, ain't you heard?" Chip gave the boy a stare, then said, over his shoulder, going around the circle, "Gordon, this is Ben, and Sweetmeat and Ricky, my cousins Josh and Joey—they're twins—and Specs, Kevin, and Catfish."

The boys weren't smiling much, but they didn't look like they wanted to fight, either. I leaned my bike against a tree, and tugged my cap down a bit tighter. I stuck my hands in my pockets.

"Catfish," Chip said to a tall boy in a Monarchs cap, "you the other captain. I got Gordon, so you get next pick."

"Ben," he said quickly, and in a minute the sides were divvied up, five players each. We walked into the lot.

"Carpet is first, bath mat is second, third is that phone book—what's left of it—and this is home," Chip said, tapping his bat on a cafeteria tray half-buried in the dirt. He looked around. "Ball goes over any fence, it's a homer. Ball goes over *that* fence—" He pointed to a tall, board fence way off in left field. "—we need to get us another ball."

Everyone chuckled at that. "Any questions?" Chip asked.

"Yeah, who died an' made *you* king?" the boy called Sweetmeat asked.

"Mr. Slugger, here." Chip tapped the bat on his shoulder. "Mr. Louis-ville Slugger."

"Fair 'nough."

Catfish pulled a nickel out of his pocket. "Call it."

"Heads," Chip said.

Catfish tossed the coin up and let it land in the dirt. "Heads it is. You up first. Let's play us some *ball*."

Their pitcher—Specs—went out to the mound, a bare patch in the scrubby grass. He was a lanky boy with black-framed glasses, the ear parts wrapped around the back of his head with electrical tape. Ricky was catcher. Chip was up first. He got a hit between second and third. Then Specs tossed three fast ones right by Joey and I was up.

Specs had a nice high leg kick, but he paused in mid-stride, so his delivery was a little jerky, like he was trying too hard to blow away the new kid. I took a ball and a strike, Ricky making the calls. The third pitch I liked. I hit it hard, but off the end of the bat. If it hadn't taken a bounce off a rock near second, I might have been out. But Josh couldn't field it, and I was safe on first.

Chip scored on Sweetmeat's long fly to left. I was stranded on third when Sweetmeat got caught trying to steal second and Kevin struck out. I walked back to the plate, picked up my glove, and took the mound.

I struck out Josh and Ben, then Catfish hit a solid

liner and made it to second, standing up. He never got any farther. I blew three sliders right by Ricky, and the inning was over.

"Not too shabby, Gordon," Specs said on his way to the mound.

Whew.

We settled into a rhythm, the teams pretty evenly matched. Chip hit one over the fence, Ben matching it the next time up. In the bottom of the fourth, tied two-all, a gust of wind came up, swirling dirt, and blew my cap off my head before I could grab it.

Josh stopped picking at the Band-Aid on his finger and stared out at the mound. "You're a *girl,*" he said.

Everyone except Chip turned and looked at me like I was Godzilla, their mouths hanging open.

"Yep," I said. I blew a big bubble of Bazooka, cool and casual.

"*Damn,*" Joey and Josh said, in one voice.

"That a problem?" Chip asked.

"Sure is," Ricky said. "I ain't playing with no—"

"—with nobody who struck out your sorry ass, swingin', three ups out of three?" Chip finished.

"You hit worse than my mama, Ricky," Kevin said.

Sweetmeat laughed. "My *grandmomma* hit better'n you."

And that was that. We kept playing. When it was my turn to bat, though, I saw Joey and Josh look at me and shake their heads, both at the same time. "Damn," they said again.

We played until Chip hit a towering two-run homer over the wrong fence, losing the last ball, and the game broke up.

"You come back," Specs said to me. "You got *style*."

I smiled. "Thanks. You got a *sweet* arm."

"I do, don't I?" He grinned and walked away, whistling, his hand slapping his glove to the rhythm.

"You wanna come over?" Chip asked. "My mom made cookies, on account'a my cousins visiting."

"Sure." I picked up my bike and walked it along the sidewalk with Chip and the twins. He turned in to the driveway of a small pale-green house.

"Lean your bike on the garage," he said. "We'll go in the back." He pointed, and when I did, he opened the door and yelled, "Ma! I'm home!" He and his cousins swarmed in.

I saw his mother step away from the sink and wipe her hands on a flowered apron. "Aloysius Bell! How many times I told you, no hollerin' in *my* house."

"Aloysius?" I asked, from the back stoop. I was trying not to laugh. No wonder he went by Chip.

He half turned. "You tell and you're dead."

I zipped a finger across my lips.

His mother put her hands on her hips. "And all three of you, hats off inside the house."

The boys looked sheepish and took off their caps. They wiped their feet on the mat, too. When they'd cleared the doorway, I came in. I wiped my feet and, after a second, took off my cap, too.

Chip's mom looked at me, and I saw her eyes get big with surprise, and her mouth had a little twitch. "Well, well, well. And who might *this* be?"

"That's Gordon," Chip said. "Um—Katy. She pitched today."

"Did she now?"

"Yes, ma'am. Struck out Joey twice."

Chip's mom had an expression on her face that I couldn't quite figure out. I wasn't sure if it was because I was white, or because I was a girl—or what. I'd seen teachers on the playground look at me that way when I headed out to the grass, like they wanted to tell me I *had* to play hopscotch with the other girls, except it wasn't an actual rule, so they couldn't. I hoped Mrs. Bell wasn't about to give me a lecture about how girls ought to behave. That'd be bad enough, but in front of guys I didn't know—?

Instead, she broke into a big smile. "Good for you, sugar. You come right in and tell me all about it." She looked at Chip. "Don't make out like you're shy when it comes to cookies. You know where they are. You boys take two each and stop messin' up my clean kitchen."

"Yes, ma'am." He and his cousins ripped across the

kitchen like their sneakers were on fire and attacked the cookie jar.

"Now take your cousins downstairs and show them those race cars you got for Christmas. This young lady and I have some things to discuss."

Chip looked at me and mouthed, "You okay?" When I shrugged, he opened the basement door, and the three of them pounded down the stairs, leaving me alone with his mom.

She patted one of the vinyl chairs. "You set yourself right down here." She put a plate of cookies on the table. I sat on the edge of the chair. I wasn't sure what was about to happen.

Mrs. Bell poured herself a cup of coffee. "So, you think you're a baseball player?"

I hesitated, nibbling the edge of a cookie, then said, "Yes—ma'am."

"Sounds like you showed those boys a thing or two."

"I guess so." I nibbled more of the cookie. It was crunchy and soft at the same time, the best kind, and was full of raisins and nuts.

"You guess?" She raised an eyebrow.

"I did get eight strikeouts, and I hit the ball over the fence once." I grinned. "They were pretty surprised."

"I bet they were." She opened their fridge and took out a carton of milk. "Cocoa?"

"Sure." I took another cookie. "I mean, yes, please."

"Good. 'Cause I got a story I think you'll want to hear." She poured the milk into a saucepan and added two scoops of Hershey's powder. "You know 'bout Hank Aaron, right?"

"Of course. He was the National League MVP this year. Everyone's heard of *him*."

"Nowadays, sure. But early in 1952, he was playin' second base for a team called the Indianapolis Clowns."

"Is that why Chip has a Clowns cap?"

"Partly. When Aaron got signed up by the Boston Braves later that year—a lot of teams were signin' colored men by then—that left second base open for the Clowns. Who do you suppose took over that position?"

I shook my head.

"My sister, that's who."

Chapter 24

Something New Every Day

"What?" I said. I was so startled I spit cookie crumbs onto the red checkered tablecloth.

"You heard me. My little sister, Toni, played second base for the Indianapolis Clowns and the Kansas City Monarchs." She stirred the cocoa, poured it into a mug, and set it down in front of me. "You heard of those teams?"

"No, ma'am."

"I didn't think so. They were part of the Negro Leagues."

Oh. That explained the other boys' caps. "How did she get the job?"

She sat down. "Sugar, she was just like you. Playin' ball with the boys as soon as she was big enough to hold a bat. My parents thought it was sinful, a girl carryin' on like that, and they tried to put a stop to it."

"Did they?"

"Nothing they could do. She'd sneak out before the sun was up and not come home 'til supper." She sipped at her coffee. "We grew up in Saint Paul—that's in Minnesota. Her real name is Marcenia, but since she was always playin' with some ragtag bunch of boys, everybody called her Tomboy."

"Did you play, too?"

"No, not me. I just ate Wheaties for her."

"Huh?"

"The cereal company had a baseball club where you could get bats and gloves with enough box tops. I didn't care two cents about baseball—or Wheaties, neither—but I ate a bowl every morning so she could get her some equipment."

"That was nice of you," I said.

"Weren't no stoppin' Tomboy once she had her mind set on a thing," Mrs. Bell said, shaking her head. "There was a big-league player who started a baseball school—only for boys, of course. Tomboy hung around for weeks asking for a chance to play."

"Did he let her?"

"Eventually. When he did, he let her in his school for free and even went out and bought her cleats with his own money. Still, it wasn't easy for her. She didn't have many friends, dropped out of school, 'cause the only thing she cared for was baseball. Then the war came, changed everything. Your daddy in the war?"

"He was. A scientist, not a soldier."

"We needed them, too. I was a nurse by then, and married, had moved out here. When it was over, Tomboy moved here, too, only now she wasn't Tomboy anymore. She called herself Toni Stone, and in '49, she got herself a job playing for the San Francisco Sea Lions."

"It's—" I bit my lip, because it's bad manners to correct a grown-up, but this was *my* team. "It's the *Seals*, Mrs. Bell. The San Francisco Seals."

"No, young lady." She waggled a finger at me, the way my gramma sometimes did. "I know all about the Seals. Fine team. The San Francisco *Sea Lions* was a colored team. Only places my people could play, before Jackie Robinson."

"Oh," I said. "I'm sorry. I didn't know."

"And now you do. Learn something new every day." She smiled. "Here's another thing maybe you don't know. They were barnstormers. You know what *that* means?"

"Uh-huh. Means they traveled all the time."

She smiled. "You know your stuff." She drank some coffee, and I took a sip of my cocoa, which had cooled off enough not to burn my tongue.

"So there they was, playing in little podunk towns and big cities, too. Now, Toni found out the manager was payin' every single one of the men players more than her, and that didn't sit right. So when they got to New Orleans, she up and left."

"Where did she go?"

"To the New Orleans Creoles. And *they*—" She stopped and looked to make sure I was paying the right sort of attention. "They paid her three *hundred* dollars a month."

"Wow."

"Yes, indeed. That was *good* money back then. The Creoles were part of the Negro Leagues, but not one of the big ones."

"A farm team?"

She thought for a moment. "I suppose so. They put her at second base, but she could *hit*, too. You should have seen that ball fly when she came up to bat."

"I woulda liked to see that," I said. I reached for another cookie, then stopped. I'd already had two, and it wasn't polite for a guest to eat up all the food.

"You go on," she said. "There's always a bunch of boys in the house, and I made plenty." She got up and poured another cup of coffee.

"Whatever happened to her? Your sister."

"She's Mrs. Alberga now, lives in Oakland, a bit more than a mile from here." She smiled. "Would you like to meet her?"

"Would I! I mean—yes, ma'am."

"All right then. Toni and her husband, Gus, are having a barbecue next weekend. He's in politics, so there'll be a mix of that and family." She tapped a finger on her napkin. "Tell you what. Give me your number. I'll call your mama to invite you, nice and proper." She reached over to the counter by the phone and handed me a little pad of paper and a pencil.

I wrote down our number, then added my mom's name, Terry, so they didn't have to call each other Mrs. So-and-So. I slid the pad back to her.

"Good. I'll call her after supper." She looked at the clock. "Speaking of which, you better scoot yourself home before it gets dark." She stood up. "I've got a casserole to make and six hungry mouths to feed."

"Okay. Thanks for the cookies. And the story." I got up and went over to the basement door. "Hey, Chip!" Sounds of scuffling stopped, and I saw him come around a corner and stand at the bottom of the stairs. "I gotta go. Thanks for letting me play and all."

"Anytime," he said, and then he was grabbed from behind by one of the cousins—I couldn't tell which one—and they started to wrestle, the way boys do when grown-ups aren't watching.

It wasn't quite dark outside. The sky to the west was all orange and pink. I rode home as fast as I could pedal, trying to keep what Mrs. Bell had told me inside my head so I could write it all down in my notebook.

The Sea Lions. The Creoles. The Clowns. Baseball might be the all-American game, but Toni Stone had played in a very different America.

Chapter 25

Best Barbecue Ever

Mom was on the phone with Mrs. Bell for a long time after dinner, long enough that I was afraid something was wrong and she was going to say no. Turned out they'd been talking about the PTA and the Co-op and other boring stuff.

The next Saturday was overcast and gray. I wanted to wear my Seals jersey, but Mom said that it wasn't a game, it was a grown-up party, and that shirt was too ragged for polite company.

"Can I wear pants?"

"I suppose. It is a barbecue. No cap."

I gave a big sigh, like that was punishment, and went back upstairs and found my almost-new corduroys and a clean shirt and my saddle shoes. I put my notebook, a pen, and my camera into my reporter bag.

Mom drove me over to Chip's house, even though it was only about half a mile. "Mrs. Bell said they'd drive you home. I didn't want your nice pants getting caught in the bicycle chain," she said. "Laundry's hard enough without adding axle grease."

When I rang the bell, Chip answered the door. He wore blue jeans and a white button-down shirt, which both looked like they'd just been ironed. Moms are all alike when it comes to party clothes. We waited in the kitchen while his dad loaded up the trunk of their Ford.

Mr. Bell was a tall man with a thin mustache. He had on a sports coat and a hat. "Ice and sodas all loaded up," he said. He picked up a wicker picnic basket from the kitchen table, and groaned like it weighed a ton. "How many beans did you make, woman?"

"Enough for two armies." Mrs. Bell turned to me. "My sister never did learn to cook. Too busy playin' ball." She pointed to the basket. "Gus, her husband, he does the barbecuing. The rest of us bring the fixin's."

The basket went into the trunk. I sat in the backseat with Chip and his brother, Oscar, who was in high school, and was so tall and skinny he had his knees tucked half-way to his chest.

The Albergas lived in a wooden house on Isabella Street in West Oakland. Mr. Bell led us up the driveway into a backyard with a picnic table and a smoky barbecue that was half the size of a car. The air smelled *really* good.

About a dozen people stood around with bottles of beer, men and women. I was the only white person. When I came in the gate, every single head turned to look at me.

I'm not exactly shy—I don't mind talking in class, or being the center of attention in a game—but this felt different. I wasn't sure what to do. Chip's mom put her hand on my shoulder, to show people I belonged with her, and said to a woman in dark pants and a print blouse, "This is Katy, Chip's friend. The ball player. Katy, this is my sister."

"Hello, little pitcher," Toni Stone said. "You got big ears?" Her voice was high and breathy, like a kid's. She sure looked like an athlete, though—tall and muscled, with thick, dark hair and gray eyes. She was older than my sisters, younger than my mom, and bounced on the balls of her feet, waiting and wary, as if a ball might come at her any minute. I knew how that felt.

"It's an honor to meet you, ma'am," I said. If I'd been wearing my cap, I would have taken it off.

"Is it now?" She turned to Chip's mom. "You been tellin' tales about me?"

"Not tales if they're true. I might have mentioned a few high points."

"I'd like to hear more," I said.

"I s'pose." She didn't seem all that happy about it. "Maybe later."

Mrs. Bell took her hand off my shoulder. "You and Chip get yourselves a plate of food and a cold drink. Once everyone's fed and the men start talking politics and cars, you'll get your chance."

"Okay. Thanks." I followed Chip and got an Orange Crush out of a big washtub full of ice and bottles of soda and beer. A woman in a red striped dress heaped my plate with potato salad and baked beans and pointed to the barbecue. "We got chicken and ribs and hot links."

"The ribs are the *best,*" Chip said. I asked for those, and a man in a porkpie hat slathered sauce all over them with a little brush.

"My mom made the sauce, too," Chip said. "Brought it over yesterday, 'cause Gus fires up the grill before breakfast." He pointed to a white-haired man wearing a coat and tie and talking very seriously to a bunch of other men.

"He your grandfather?" I asked.

"Nope. That's Gus. Uncle Pescia. He's Aunt Toni's husband."

"Really? He's so old."

"Yep. He turned seventy year before last. There was a party." Chip sat down at the picnic table. "He was the first colored man to be an officer in the U.S. Army." He took a bite of ribs. "World War One," he mumbled through a mouth full of food.

Those ribs were the best I'd ever eaten. The sauce was

smoky and tangy, and the meat was so tender it fell off the bones. Even the potato salad tasted better. I went back for seconds before I got too stuffed to move.

Chip's mom and another woman went inside to get the desserts. Most of the men stood over by the fence, smoking and arguing. The air was almost blue with puffing and gesturing with cigarettes and cigars. They'd get really loud, and then one of them would bust out laughing.

"Where'd your Aunt Toni go?" I asked.

"Prob'ly down to the basement. She's not real sociable." He finished his soda—his second—and burped, "Dwight—!"

"Why'd you say that?"

"Me and my cousins have a bet. Josh says he can burp the president's whole entire name—Dwight David Eisenhower. I've never heard him do it. Far as I can ever get is Dwight." He pointed toward the house. "Ask my mom where Aunt Toni went."

"You sure?"

"Yeah. I don't mind sittin' here. Oscar'll be done pretending he's a grown-up pretty soon."

"Okay." I picked up my bag. The kitchen had a yellow linoleum floor and smelled like baking, and soap from the dishes. Chip's mom was washing up while another woman cut a cake into pieces. Covering the table was a cherry pie, a plate of brownies, and a bowl of fruit salad.

A third woman stood at the counter with an eggbeater, whipping cream into frothy peaks. None of them were Toni Stone.

The whipped cream woman touched Chip's mom's arm. "Bunny?"

She turned around. "Hey there. You get enough to eat?"

"Yes, ma'am," I said. "It was great. Especially the potato salad."

"Thank you kindly," said the woman cutting the pie. "That's my specialty. I'll even tell you my secret. I use brown mustard. Not that nasty yellow kind."

"I'll tell my mom." I would, too. It was *great* potato salad. "Is Ton—? Is Mrs.— ?" Rats. I couldn't remember her married last name. "Is Tomboy around?" I hoped that was okay.

"She in the basement, lookin' at her past glory," the pie woman said. "Rememberin' who she used to be." She pointed at a door. "Go on down. Sometime she likes it when young folks want to talk baseball. Maybe you can cheer her up a bit."

"I'll try." I took the stairs two at a time. The basement smelled musty. It was lit with bare bulbs hanging from the ceiling over a wringer washer and piles of busted furniture. Stacks of newspapers were bound up with twine, and I had to turn sideways to get past a big old cabinet radio.

At the far end of the room, Toni Stone sat in a straight-back chair behind a table with half a dozen shoeboxes and thick photo albums. A brown bottle that said JIM BEAM and a half-full jelly glass stood next to an open scrapbook. She looked up when she heard my footsteps.

"I was wonderin' if you were gonna come down and see me." She patted the top of a big wooden barrel. "Sit. Take a load off."

I sat.

"Whad'ya think of that?" She pointed to the page.

"Wow." A piece of yellowed newspaper had a picture of her, much younger, in a baseball uniform, with a big-letter headline:

NEW ORLEANS LADY SACK IS SENSATION OF SOUTHERN LEAGUE

"That was in 1949," she said. "I played second base for the New Orleans Creoles. My daddy 'bout dropped his teeth when he opened up the *Chicago Defender* and saw his wayward daughter, big as life." She ran a finger along the edge of the clipping. "You ever heard of the *Chicago Defender*?"

"Uh-uh." I tried to read the tiny print underneath the picture.

"Most important colored paper in the whole United States. And there I am." She sipped from the jelly glass.

"That season we had a game with the Black Barons, out of Birmingham. They had this young rookie, barely eighteen." She looked up at me. "You may have heard of him. Willie Mays?"

"No kidding? You played against Willie Mays?"

"Hah. Back then, Willie was gobsmacked to play against *me*. I was pretty darn famous." She patted the stack of scrapbooks.

"I'll say." I pulled out my notebook. "Do you mind if I write some of this down?"

"Be my guest. I've had my share of reporters hangin' around. You work for your school paper?"

"No, ma'am. It's a project for my class." I clicked open my pen. "How did you start out?"

"Same as you, I reckon. Playin' sandlot with the boys. That didn't make me popular with the other girls, but I didn't care, as long as I got to play. Then I got on a team in the Catholic League in Saint Paul."

"Did those boys make a fuss?"

"Some. Called me names, told me to go home, play with my dollies, be a *girl*." She made a face. "I had to let it wash over me. The price of playin'. One thing I *did* mind? The coaches taught the boys how to turn a double play, how to slide. Paid no attention to me. Prob'ly hoped I would give up and go on home."

"You didn't, did you?"

"No, I did not. I got myself a copy of the rule book, and

I studied it—a lot more than I did my schoolwork—and went to the library and read every book they had about baseball. After a bit, I knew more than any boy on the team, and that riled them up some."

"They were mad at you?"

"Nope. They was *scared.* Never met a girl like me, and it shook them. Some of their folks thought I was a menace to society." She grinned. "I 'spect you know what I'm talkin' about, don't you?"

"Yep," I said. I got that goose bump feeling again. "I sure do."

Chapter 26

The End of an Era

I told her my story. By now I could do it in a couple of sentences, not take up the whole conversation, which is important when you're talking to somebody really interesting.

"The Little League wasn't around when I was your age," Toni Stone said. "I did play American Legion ball. They had the same kind of rule about girls, but my coach paid it no mind. Once he saw me in the infield, I wasn't a girl, just another player."

"You're lucky," I said.

She gave me a sharp, hard look. "I worked for it. Showed up, every day, no matter what." She sat back in her chair a little. "I guess there's luck, too. Right person comes to the right game, you better hope your bat and your glove got that magic."

"At least they let you play."

"Most times. But you listen here—wasn't only the boys shut me out. As soon as I read about that girls' league during the war, I wrote and asked for a tryout."

"Which team were you on?" I wondered if she knew Deb Kilgallen.

"None of them. They turned me down flat, sight unseen."

"What? How come?"

"*That* league only signed white girls."

"Oh." I looked down at my hands. "I didn't know that."

"Not something they said out loud much."

We sat there for a minute in silence. I didn't know what to say. Finally I asked, "So where *did* you play?"

"Well, after Jackie Robinson, the majors started cherry-picking from the Negro Leagues. Worked out for me. When Hank Aaron went to the Braves, I got his spot on the Clowns." She opened another scrapbook and flipped through the pages, then put her finger on a flyer.

I leaned over and read.

TONI STONE:
THE GAL GUARDIAN OF SECOND BASE

"Most folks thought it was a publicity stunt," she said, "having a 'gal' ball player, like one team had got itself a dwarf. The manager wanted me to wear a skirt, show off my woman-ness. I told him I played *base*ball, and if he wanted a freak show, I'd quit. He gave me a regular uniform, but most days I still felt like a goldfish, everyone staring at me like I had two heads."

"That sounds awful," I said. I knew how that felt, too, but only with a handful of guys, not thousands.

"I had some real bad days, but I took my knocks without whinin'. Part of the deal." She took a sip from her glass. "I wanted to prove I was the best damn ball player they'd ever seen—not *lady* ball player, just straight-up best."

She turned the pages, slow enough that I could read the newspaper headlines, page after page, with posters and flyers and photos—every one of them about Toni Stone. I took my camera out of the canvas bag. "Is it okay if I take pictures of some of the articles? To go with my report?"

"I don't mind, but your pictures won't come out too good in this light." She reached for one of the cardboard boxes. "I tell you what. When I first played with the Clowns, the manager had me go to the stands, sell pictures of myself, after the game." She frowned. "I didn't like that one bit. But now I'm glad of it. Shows me in my uniform, shows I was a *ball* player." She gave me a big, glossy photo, her signature in black ink across the bottom.

There she was, leaping off the bag, a ball in her glove, caught like a bird in mid-flight.

"You were famous!"

"Yes, I was. Until big-league integration started killing the Negro Leagues—ain't *that* a kick in the gut? Every year, the stands got emptier. I hated all the publicity—film crews and magazines and reporters acted like they all came to see a circus act, not a baseball game." She shook her head. "Still, publicity means fans, and fans mean scouts. I had a dream—a big one. I was gonna be the first woman to play in the majors."

"Did the scouts come?"

"They sure did. And they saw I was batting .300, fielding line drives, turning double plays that the *guys* whistled at. I played with some of the best in the world—hell, I got a hit off of Satchel Paige himself."

"Zowie."

She smiled and flipped a few more pages. "Thing was, the manager'd *start* me—I was who the crowd came to see—then around the bottom of the third, when I wasn't a *surprise* no more, he'd take me out and I'd ride the bench the rest of the game. That hurt my stats." She tapped a box score on a piece of newspaper, turning the scrapbook so I could read the tiny print.

"You were *really* good."

"I was loads better than that. Half my numbers never made the books. Little places we played, papers only came out once a week, and if that was the day we hit town, no one recorded the game. One of our guys usually kept score, but if he left his book on the bus, whole games—whole road trips—just got lost."

I copied down some of the headlines in my notebook. "It still sounds exciting."

"Some days. It was a tough life, bein' a colored ball player. A night game in one town, then sleepin' on the bus 'til we got to the next one. Places down south, we had sardines and crackers for dinner on the side of the road, 'cause no restaurant would serve us. One diner that did, when I was walking out the door, I heard a crash. I turned around and saw that waitress smashing plates to the floor."

"She broke her *own* dishes?"

"Some white folks—well, let's just say there ain't enough soap and hot water to clean off the touch of a colored person's mouth, for them. If a dog had eaten off those plates, I bet she'd have washed them, lickety-split."

"That's terrible," I said, one hand clenched in a fist. "But it was a long time ago, right?"

She shook her head. "Not even five years. Still happening today. You know 'bout those children in Little Rock?"

"Uh-huh. We talked about them a lot, for Current Events."

"You think 'current' mean a long time ago?"

"No. The opposite."

"That's right. I bet a lot of dishes gonna get busted up

in that school's cafeteria 'fore things settle down." She sighed. "Crowds called me names, threw stuff. I had to grow a mighty thick skin." She looked off into the shadows of the basement. After a long moment, she looked back at me.

"I was the most famous woman baseball player in the world. There was going to be a Louisville Slugger bat with my autograph."

"Cool. Can I see it?"

"Never happened. Mr. Louisville put the kibosh on it. Even after *Ebony* magazine did a whole article about me." She opened the last scrapbook and turned it toward me. "July of 1953."

There were four pages, all with pictures. "That's amazing," I said. I wished our library had back issues of *that* magazine.

"Seemed like it, at first. A reporter and a photographer following me around, watching me play, asking all kinds of questions—shoo-ey."

Her voice didn't sound happy.

"But—?"

"But turned out more jive than truth, and I was sorry I ever said yes. Read that part." She held a long brown finger against the pale paper. "Read it out loud for me."

I did. "'Toni Stone is an attractive young woman who could be someone's secretary.'" I made a face. "Did they think that was a *compliment*?"

"They tried to make out that I was a *lady* who just happened to play ball. It's all light and la-de-da. Like one day I put down my pots and pans and accidentally picked up a bat and—" She made a *pfftt* sound.

I bit my lip and looked down at my notes. "Why did you retire?"

"Things changed. The Clowns hired two more women. Mamie Johnson—she was a pitcher, and a good one, and so tiny everyone called her Peanut. And Connie Morgan. She was eighteen, and she played second base."

"Wait. That was your position."

"Yep. Connie was a sweet young thing, and I had rough hands and a sort of bowlegged walk. I was thirty-three by then, which is the old-folks home in baseball. More and more, the manager put Connie in and benched me."

"So you left?"

"Not quite yet. The '54 season, I signed with the Kansas City Monarchs. The greatest colored baseball team in the world. Jackie Robinson, Satchel Paige, Ernie Banks—they all played there one time or another."

"Wow."

"I'll say. Kansas City was good times. Baseball, jazz, and the fellas took me serious. Not everyone did." She flipped a few more pages. "Like this man, in the *Chicago Defender*, no less. No help at all."

> The entire social order could be toppled if women like Toni Stone are allowed to keep playing baseball. Her presence threatens men's morale and makes them feel "pretty silly."

I frowned. "That's exactly what Little League said. That girls playing would distract boys from the game."

"Bull. The trouble was, the Negro Leagues was on its last legs. Folks could turn on the tee-vee for free, see more'n a dozen colored players by then." She took another sip of her drink. "Things had gone a little different, I might have been the first woman in the majors."

"Did you ever get a contract?"

"Nope. A white gal almost did, though. Eleanor Engle, back in 1952."

I made a face. "I know about *her*."

Toni Stone nodded. "That poor gal sat in the dugout in her nice new uniform, never even got up to bat once. Next day, both the majors and minors set a rule: no women. Couldn't even try out. *Women. Could. Not. Play.*" She banged her hand on the table with each word.

"That sucks eggs."

"Ain't that the truth. After that, there was no place for me to go from the Monarchs, no matter how good I played. End of that season, I hung up my cleats and came home to Gus."

I sat, silent, for a long time. I could hear water dripping somewhere, and the sounds of the women upstairs in the kitchen, laughing. Toni Stone's story was exactly what I'd been hoping for—except for a happy ending. "Little League's never going to let me play, are they?" I asked with a sigh.

"Prob'ly not. It's the menfolks in their fancy suits that controls the contracts and the money. That's the way things always been."

"The 'status quo,' my mom says."

"She's a smart lady." Toni Stone closed her scrapbooks, one at a time. "I tell you, at first, not playing hurt so bad I thought my heart would bust from the wanting of it. But look here, child. Yesterday, I played a pickup game, over at the park. Felt good. Hit one over the fence, and tagged a swift young buck out at first. Shoulda seen the look on that boy's face." She smiled. "I may not have a team, or a uniform, but I am *mighty* fond of my glove."

"Me too."

"*Nobody* can take that away." She looked at me. "When that Little League said no, you give up baseball?"

I shook my head. "I play with the neighborhood guys. And Chip, now."

"See. There's always a game somewhere. This spring I'm going to start a young folks' league at my church, keep my hand in on the basics, maybe scout some new talent. Like you?"

"I could try out?" If Little League didn't change their minds, it felt nice to know there might be *some*where I could learn to play better.

"You can *always* try." She stood up and stretched. "Playing in the majors? That door slammed in my face. Still, me on the Clowns, that opened one for Peanut and Connie. Who knows what'll happen. Ten, fifteen years from now, maybe I'll read about *you* pitching for the Giants."

"I'd like that." From the way baseball had treated *her*, it didn't seem real likely, but the idea made me smile.

"You know, sugar, I would, too." Toni Stone reached up for the cord and turned off the light.

Chapter 27

My American Heroes

"Are stamps school supplies?"

"Depends." Mom stubbed out her cigarette. "What do you need to mail?"

I held up a handful of envelopes. "Letters to women baseball players. For my project."

"You found that many?" She looked surprised.

"I found *hundreds*," I said. "And *no*body knows about them."

"Why not?"

"Got me. Some of them played for more than *twenty* years." I put the stack of envelopes down. "You keep up with the news, right?"

"I try."

"Have you ever heard about any women playing baseball?"

Mom thought for a minute, then shook her head.

"See. It's like everything about them just got—erased."

"Is all this going into your report?"

"You betcha."

"Sounds like school supplies to me." She opened her purse and gave me three quarters, enough for two dozen three-cent stamps.

By the end of January, I'd gotten replies from all but three of the women. The letters were friendly. Some were only half a page; others were long and full of stories. I got ten autographed photos, a couple of old ticket stubs, even a felt pennant. I used my Christmas money to buy my own scrapbook, with a red leather cover and lots of black paper pages, for the pieces I'd want to save forever.

My project had grown from an essay to a whole display, way, way more than Mr. H had asked for. I knew that. But I was hooked. I wanted to keep looking until I found every woman who'd ever played, not for my grade, but because I was curious, and I was the only kid who seemed to care.

Still, my school project was due the next week. It was time to pick out my favorites and actually *do* the report. I laid everything out on the table in the attic: letters, photographs, newspaper clippings, photocopies of articles, souvenirs. The only thing I didn't have were baseball cards. There weren't any for *these* players. I'd have to make my own.

The dime store had a box of Topps cards on the counter. I paid my nickel and chewed the flat pink slab of gum while I sorted through the pack. I didn't care who was on the card. I just wanted the right look for my homemade ones.

I'd found a pantograph in Suze's nest of art supplies, a sort of foldout ruler. When I traced part of a card with the blunt end, a pencil at the other end automatically drew the exact same shape on a blank sheet of paper, three times as big. A full-page baseball card.

I used the lettering stencil to make the players' names at the top of each one look like they were printed. Mom let me type up all the other information I had—stats, team names, dates. Then I cut up the paper, and rubber-cemented the pieces into the empty rectangles I'd colored in.

Jules came over and kept me company for the craft-project part. She brought her transistor radio, and while my glue dried we danced around to KOBY playing "Peggy Sue" and "Great Balls of Fire."

It took me a while to pick out which women I wanted to use. To meet Mr. H's very high standards, I needed ones who did more than just play ball. Ones who were the first, who broke down barriers and opened doors. I got it down to twelve, arranging them from oldest to newest, starting in 1898 and ending in 1954. Lizzie Arlington. Alta Weiss. Lizzie Murphy. Maud Nelson.

Jackie Mitchell. Edith Houghton. Babe Didrikson. Sophie Kurys. Dorothy Kamenshek. Eleanor Engle. Toni Stone. Mamie "Peanut" Johnson.

I worked on it every spare minute. I made twelve baseball-card "posters," with photos, if I had them, or copies of old-time drawings from newspapers and magazines, if I didn't. That part was pretty fun. Writing an essay about *why* they were my heroes was harder.

I crumpled up paper and crossed out sentences and started over. And over. By Saturday afternoon, I thought I had it, except for a title. Trying to describe my whole project in a few words was harder than I thought. The headlines on articles about the Girls' Baseball League, or the ones about Toni Stone, had been cute, or girly, or jokey, and I didn't want that.

After another hour of crumpled paper I decided to leave that part for last, and showed the rest to Mom. She sat at the kitchen table, reading it, not saying a word. When she looked up, her eyes were shiny. "I don't think I've ever been as proud of any of my girls as I am right now."

"Even when Suze got her MFA? Or Dewey got her patent?"

"Okay, it might be a three-way tie." She smiled. "I don't want to play favorites." She tapped her pen on the pile of pages. "It really is great, sweetie. I think your teacher will be thrilled. Maybe it'll convince Little League, too."

"I doubt it." I opened a bottle of Dr Pepper. "I think

the men that run Little League *want* people to believe baseball is only for boys." I patted the top page of my report. "It's more convenient if they pretend none of this ever happened." I put my hands over my ears. "La-la-la, la-la-la."

"You're awfully skeptical for a kid your age," Mom said. "Although I suppose you *were* raised by wolves. Three wolves. None of us wild, just a little odd." She took off her glasses. "I have a hankering for Chinese food. How 'bout you?"

"Hungry wolves." My stomach rumbled in agreement.

Full of sweet-and-sour pork and egg rolls, after dinner I wrote out a clean final copy of my essay. I put all the sheets into a paper folder and—fifteen minutes before bedtime—finally stenciled a title onto the cover in bold black ink.

WOMEN IN BASEBALL
America's Forgotten History

On the second Monday in February, Mr. H stood in front of his desk, holding a shoebox. "Today we'll start our presentations. There are thirty of you, so we'll do six reports a day—three in the morning, three in the afternoon. Do I have a volunteer to go first?"

Everyone looked around. Complete silence. No hands went up.

Mr. H smiled. "I was prepared for that." He held up the box. "Thirty names, thirty slips of paper, drawn at random." He reached in, shuffled them with his fingers, and pulled one out. "Chip," he announced. "You're up."

Chip's hero was a man named W. E. B. Du Bois, the first Negro to get a PhD at Harvard. He helped start the NAACP in 1909. Chip took about ten minutes to tell us about him. When he finished, he stood there for a moment, then took a little bow. Everyone clapped.

"Nice work, Chip," Mr. H said. "Please leave your report on my desk and return to your seat." He drew another slip of paper. "Mike?"

Mike did Jonas Salk, the polio vaccine scientist.

I learned a lot that week. There were the usual history guys—Lincoln, Ben Franklin, Thomas Edison. From our century, Eleanor, Franklin, and Teddy Roosevelt. Amelia Earhart and Audie Murphy. Madge Malinowsky did Emma Lazarus, who wrote the poem that's on the Statue of Liberty. Joyce Chen chose Anna May Wong, the first Chinese movie star in Hollywood. We got Davy Crockett and Daniel Boone, Harriet Tubman and Jesse Owens, and Jackie Robinson—twice.

I'd been a little scared that I was the only one who'd done a *sports* report, so those were good to hear. Mr. H shook his head when Pinky started his talk—he'd picked Joe Shuster and Jerry Siegel, the men who invented Superman. Then Pinky made a pretty good point about Superman being *the* symbol of truth, justice, and the American way, and after, Mr. H gave him a smile and a nod.

Not everyone's hero was famous. Andy's was his dad, who had fought Nazis in France in World War II, and Danny picked his uncle, who lost a leg fighting the Japanese on Iwo Jima.

The next day, Mr. H drew PeeWee's name.

He got up and stood at the front of the class. I could see his hands shaking.

"My hero is my Jiji, my grandfather, Takayuki Ishikawa. He owned a flower shop on Ashby Ave. Now it's a bakery. You've all probably been in there and bought doughnuts. My family does *not* shop there." He took a deep breath, and talked a little slower. "That's because the government—the American government—made Jiji give up his business and his house. He was born in California, like most of us. He was an American citizen. But in the 1940s, America was at war with Japan. A lot of people thought that anyone who looked like him might be the enemy. In 1943, President Roosevelt signed a law, and 120,000 Japanese were rounded up, all over the West Coast. More than a thousand of them lived in Berkeley. Jiji and his family were loaded onto a bus that took them to Tanforan, the racetrack. They had to live in a stable. My mother finished high school in a concentration camp in the desert called Manzanar."

The room was silent. I couldn't even hear anyone breathing. PeeWee continued for another five minutes. He was almost crying by the end. Mr. H came up and put an arm around his shoulders for a second. "You've given us all a lot to think about—what it means to be American, what it means to be a hero."

He looked out at the class. "How many of you knew about this part of our history?"

Only Sam Yakimora and Gloria Fong raised their hands.

"And yet it happened right here in your hometown, only *fifteen* years ago. That's before any of you were born, but—" He shook his head. "We'll talk more about the internment next week. It's important to remember that terrible things can happen, even here."

Then Mr. H did something I'd never seen a teacher do. He stepped back and bowed, from the waist, very formal. "Thank you, Katsuharo-san."

PeeWee looked as startled as the rest of us. Then he bowed back, and handed Mr. H his report.

There were only five slips left when Mr. H reached in on Friday morning and called my name. My stomach did a little flip-flop as I walked up to his desk.

I'd practiced at home, after a few kids got tongue-tied, standing up there with their mouths open like fish, or reading their reports with their heads down, mumbling—fast—to get through. I wasn't exactly scared—people watched me all the time when I was pitching—but I needed to get this *right*.

I started by telling my own story. "Most of you have seen me out on the playground, playing baseball. You might think I'm a little strange, because baseball is a boy's game. You probably think I'm the only girl who's ever played. But you'd be wrong."

I told them about my research, and about each of my heroes, holding up their posters, one at a time. When I laid Mamie Johnson down on the desk in front of me, I looked out at my classmates.

"All year, we've talked about civil rights. No discrimination because of race or religion. We haven't talked much about men and women. In our classroom, during math and science, Mr. H makes sure girls have the same opportunities as boys. But that's not true in gym, or on the playground. There, girls *are* separate. We're not even taught the same games."

I tapped the papers in front of me. "These women did not have equal opportunities. They were blacklisted by baseball, not because they were communists, but because they *weren't* men. That didn't stop them. They kept playing, they kept trying. No one's ever heard of most of them. But each of them has a story. And they're *my* American heroes."

For a minute, there was no sound in the room. I looked over at Mr. H. He sat on the edge of his desk, staring at me. Finally someone—I think it was PeeWee—started to clap, and I took my bow. I straightened the pages, put them back in the folder, and laid it on Mr. H's desk.

"Well done, Katy," he said. "Well done indeed."

At lunch a bunch of guys came up to my table. "Was any of that for real?" Matt asked.

"Every bit of it."

"Jeez-Louise," he said, shaking his head.

That kept happening, all afternoon, kids coming up and asking questions. Baseball wasn't my secret anymore. I wasn't a weirdo, I was part of a long tradition. That felt pretty darn good.

Monday morning, class started with the usual Current Events. The Pope declared St. Clare the patron saint of television. The United States had finally launched a satellite on the last day of January, Explorer 1. It was an army rocket, from my dad's project in Alabama. I guess I should have been more excited, because of that, but it seemed like America was just playing catch-up, not doing anything brand-new, like Sputnik last fall. The news I really wanted to hear was what grade I'd get on my report. Mr. H told us he was reading them all, and would give them back in a week or so.

The next Wednesday, half an hour before the afternoon bell, he set a cardboard box on his desk.

"I was very impressed by your projects," he said. "Most of you did excellent research and presented your findings in an interesting, organized manner." He started pulling reports out of the box, stacking them on his desk in seven piles. One pile was much smaller than the others. "You introduced us to many courageous men and women, some familiar, some not.

"When the bell rings, you can come up and get your reports. They're organized by table." He patted one of the stacks. "First, however—" He paused and waited until the whole room was quiet. "I've been teaching for five years, and I have never given *any*one an A-plus." He smiled. "Until now. And today, I'm giving two."

Gasps, all around the room.

"PeeWee, you gave us a much-needed civics lesson. You showed us that we should never take our freedom for granted." He walked over to PeeWee's desk and handed him his report. "A-plus."

The other folder he was holding was mine.

"And Katy. You uncovered a history *none* of us knew anything about. That's the kind of research a college student would be proud of." He gave me my report, a big red A+ on the cover.

"Katy, PeeWee, with your permission, I'd like to share your work with the rest of the school, and display these in the glass case in the hallway."

"Um, yeah, okay." PeeWee looked as stunned as I felt.

I just nodded. I was numb and tingling, both. There were almost 400 students at LeConte Elementary School. Maybe seeing my heroes would change their ideas about what girls could do. One boy at a time, now one *kid* at a time. Even better.

Chapter 28

Dinner with the Bergs

A week later, I was in the cloakroom of room 120, getting my jacket, when Jules came up behind me and tapped me on the shoulder. I jumped and dropped my math book. It hit the floor with a *thump*.

"Sorry." She picked it up and handed it back. "You're invited for dinner at my house tonight."

"It's a school night. You know how my mom gets."

"Have her call mine. You'll see," Jules said. She sounded pretty sure of herself.

I pushed open the door to the playground. "Okay." Her mom was really strict, but she was a *great* cook. She didn't use mixes or cans or anything. "Some kind of special occasion?" It wasn't a holiday that I knew about, and Jules's birthday was months ago.

"Sort of." She fiddled with her hair, wrapping a curl

around her finger and then letting it twang loose again. She did that when she was nervous. Or excited. "My dad wants to talk to you."

I bit my lip. That sounded serious. "Am I in trouble at your house?" It wouldn't be the first time. But never with her *dad*.

"Nope." Jules had a funny look on her face, smiling, but trying not to, like she had a secret and couldn't wait to tell it.

"Spill the beans, Burger."

"My lips are sealed."

We got to the corner of Russell and Hillegass, where we always said good-bye. Jules lived halfway up that block. "Come over at five thirty," she said.

"That's almost two hours."

"I know. But I've got a piano lesson until five. And if you get all your homework done—"

"My mom'll have *zero* reason to say no. Gotcha." I shifted my books from one arm to the other. "You gonna at least give me a hint?"

"Nope." She shook her head, smiling big-time now. "But—my mom's making her fried chicken."

"I'll be there!" My mouth watered. Jules walked away. Strolled. After about ten feet she waved to me over her shoulder without turning around.

Why would Mr. Berg want to talk to me? At my house I changed into jeans and a sweater and got a Dr Pepper and a *small* handful of pretzels to get me through my homework. Mom had office hours Wednesday afternoons and wouldn't be home for another hour. I laid out pens and paper on the kitchen table, opened my math book to the story problems for tomorrow, and pulled a ditto sheet out of my notebook.

Mr. H always made the vocabulary words fit Current Events. This week they were all related to satellites: *gravitational, perigee, atmospheric, radiation*. We had to define them *and* use them in a sentence. It wasn't too hard, because those had been in the news all month. The United States had launched a second satellite, also called Vanguard. That was good. But then our next one, Explorer 2, fizzed out before it got into orbit. So the space race was still tied: Russia 2, America 2.

I'd finished my ten words and was on the third story problem when I heard the front door open. "In the kitchen," I yelled. I started scribbling numbers into my notebook so I'd look like I was busy and studious and all that.

"Getting a head start today?" Mom asked. She put her briefcase down on a chair with a thump.

I finished another problem. "The Bergs invited me over for dinner."

Mom frowned. "On a school night?"

"I know. But Jules says her dad wants to talk to me."

"About what?"

"Got me." I tapped my pencil on the word ARITHMETIC

at the bottom of my textbook. "She said you can call her mom and ask."

"I think I will." Mom was on the phone for a minute or two. All I heard was "Oh" and "I see" and "Well, in *that* case." When she hung up, she was smiling, the same I-know-something-you-don't-know smile that Jules had. Seemed like *every*one knew, except me.

"You're good to go," was all she said. She got a beer out of the fridge. "Be home by eight. It's still a school night."

"Will *you* tell me what this is all about?"

"Nope. I'm going to get out of these shoes and run a nice hot bath." She headed for the stairs, whistling.

What was going on?

I finished my math and read the geography section about Cuba, which was short and boring, all about coffee and sugarcane. A bunch of Current Events were happening there, but they were all *too* current to be in a textbook.

When the clock said 5:20, I closed all my books, grabbed my coat, and headed out the door.

I didn't exactly *run* to Jules's house, but I didn't walk, either. I knocked, then let myself in the back door. Jules and I had known each other forever, and I was sort of an honorary Berg.

"Hello, Katy." Mrs. Berg stood by the stove, wearing an apron with little red pots and pans on it, like June Cleaver. The kitchen smelled great. "Juliana's in the living room," she said. She shooed me off with one hand, stirring a pot of yellow sauce with the other.

Jules sat on the floor reading a Nancy Drew book. Her beagle puppy, Schubert, lay flopped on her lap. Her family named pets after musicians. They used to have a parakeet named Puccini. My family did the same thing, with scientists. My middle name was Curie, and when I was little, we had a cat named Rutherford.

"Schubert's not allowed up on the couch," she said.

"Okay." I sat down on her other side. The puppy made a grumbly sound, but didn't move. "Is that one any good?" I asked.

"They're all about the same. Nancy has adventures, her chums get into trouble, Ned rescues them all, and the mystery gets solved along the way." She bookmarked her place and closed the book. Another difference between her family and mine. We just folded down the corner of the page. Unless it was a library book, of course.

"Oh. So *now* will you tell me?"

"Nope. Daddy'll be home any minute. Hold your horses. Like this." She got up, went to the piano, and played the first part of the Lone Ranger song.

I laughed. That was our favorite song from second grade, when we were cowboys. For Christmas—and Hanukkah—that year we got matching hats and fringed red vests with white pictures of guns. Mom gave me a belt with a holster and a silver cap gun with turquoise handles that made the neighborhood boys jealous.

Right in the middle of the fast part of the song, the front door opened. "Greetings, all. Your lord and master has returned to his castle." Mr. Berg was a pudgy man with dark hair, silver-rimmed glasses, and a booming voice.

Jules ran over and gave him a hug. He patted her cheek. "Hello, princess." He took his hat off and put it down on top of a stack of mail. "Glad you could make it, Katy."

I wanted to ask, "So, what's up?" but that sounded rude. "Thanks for inviting me," I said instead.

He chuckled. "I suppose you're wondering why."

"Maybe a little." I tried to sound cool.

"Hah!" Jules said. "She can hardly stand the suspense."

"Well then, let me pour myself a drink, and we'll go into my den and have a little chat."

My face must have looked as worried as I felt, because he chuckled again and said, "It's not the Spanish Inquisition." He pulled the glass stopper from a big decanter and poured an inch of brown liquid into a glass. He motioned with his other arm. "After you, girls."

Jules and I weren't allowed in her dad's den. I'd only been in there once—to get pipe cleaners for a school project. It was the only room in their house that was even a little messy, mostly stacks of papers. He sat down in the big leather chair and pointed to the bay window. "Have a seat."

The cushion let out a little hiss of air when I sat down.

I had no idea what was coming, but it felt serious, so I sat up straight, my hands in my lap.

"I picked Juliana up from school the other day, and she showed me your display. You did a *lot* of research. I was impressed."

"Thanks." I relaxed, a little.

"I've been in the newspaper business for close to twenty years now, and had no inkling about what you discovered." He took a sip of his drink. "Women baseball players. Who knew?"

"Almost nobody," I said. "That's the problem. It's like they've just disappeared."

"So I gather." He took another drink, then cleared his throat. "How would you like to reach a larger audience, let more people in on the secret?"

"Sure. How?"

He tented his hands together. "Well, baseball fever is big right now, with the Giants coming. Every paper is looking for a new angle. My daughter thinks you've found one, and I agree. So at our Monday afternoon meeting, I pitched the idea to my boss at the *Gazette*, and he gave me the green light."

"To do what?" I was a little confused.

"Interview you. I'd ask about your research, about your female heroes, maybe even about your own baseball story. Juliana told me about Little League, says you got a raw deal."

"You can say that again," Jules chimed in.

"You want to put me in the *paper*?"

"That's the plan. I have a tape recorder here. We can talk for a while after dinner. If you have—"

He stopped when Mrs. Berg appeared in the doorway. "Supper's ready," she said.

Mr. Berg finished his drink and stood up. "So, Katy, are you game?"

"You betcha." I gave him a thumbs-up.

"Maybe that'll goose Little League, huh?" Jules whispered on the way to the dining room.

"Crossing my fingers," I said. I'd asked Mr. H to make a copy of my project before it went up in the hall, so I could send it to Little League. But I hadn't, yet. I couldn't shake the feeling that nothing was going to change their minds, and mailing all those pages would take a *lot* of stamps. I wasn't sure it was worth it. But maybe now—?

Mrs. Berg's fried chicken is the best there is, and she made macaroni, too—with *real* cheese, not boxed orange powder. I was too excited to eat much.

"Looks like someone's anxious to get started," Mrs. Berg said. "I'll make up a plate for you to take home." She looked at her husband. "Want me to keep yours warm, Ralph?"

"I intend to finish my drumstick," he said.

Five minutes later, he pushed his chair back. "Let's give this a go." He carried his chair into the den so I could sit right near his desk, then opened a small suitcase. Inside was a two-reel tape recorder. He put on a blank reel and threaded the flat, shiny brown tape through the rollers. Then he set up a little silver microphone on a black stand.

"Say your name and address, as a test," he said.

I did. He rewound the tape and played it back. My voice sounded funny, like it wasn't quite me.

He asked me questions, and I answered. After a few minutes, I forgot about the recorder, and we just talked. When the reel was almost empty, he turned off the machine and smiled at me.

"You really know your history," he said, rewinding. "I'll get my secretary to transcribe this. I may have some follow-up questions this weekend." He removed the reel. "Juliana says you have some photographs?"

"I have a whole scrapbook now. I can bring it over, if you want."

"Excellent. I think this is going to interest a lot of people, Katy."

"I hope so."

"So do I." He looked at the clock. "What do you know? Just enough time for a slice of homemade chocolate cake before I need to walk you home."

I smiled. Except for sitting on a chair with plastic covers, I liked eating dinner with the Bergs.

Chapter 29

A Giant Surprise

Saturday afternoon, Jules and I stopped at my house on our way back from the movies—*The Monolith Monsters* and *The Amazing Colossal Man*—to get my scrapbook and glove. Her dad looked at every page, and wrote down a bunch of notes in a little black book. He had a big newspaperman camera and took pictures of me holding the scrapbook open or wearing my glove. I'd asked him if he wanted me to put on my jersey and cap. He said no, it was better if I looked like an ordinary girl.

Then I waited. The paperboy delivered the *Chronicle* every morning, so we didn't usually read the *Gazette*. On the way to school, I asked Jules when the article would be published.

"I don't know," she said. "Daddy'll tell us."

Nothing, all week. The *Gazette* didn't come out on

Sundays. The next Tuesday was a gray, rainy day. I carried my books underneath my hooded slicker and wore galoshes over my saddle shoes. I met Jules at our corner. She had an umbrella and what looked like a log wrapped in a whole roll of Saran Wrap.

She pointed to the log. "You're on page seventeen," she said.

"Really?" My voice squeaked like a cartoon mouse. I wanted to look, right then, but my hands were full, and a newspaper's not easy to read on the sidewalk. Besides, it would get soggy in nothing flat. She tucked the log under my arm, and we got to school five minutes before the bell.

I hung up my slicker and kicked my galoshes off. Underneath the plastic wrap, the newspaper was clean and dry, rolled up like it would be for a paperboy to throw. I spread it out on my desk. It was so big it flopped over on three sides.

I figured I'd be in the Sports section, so I just stared when I got to page 17. At the top it said *Women's World*. Down in the corner was a tiny picture of me with my glove. The headline said:

LOCAL GIRL UNCOVERS BASEBALL SECRETS

Kathleen "Katy" Gordon, a fifth grader at LeConte Elementary School, recently surprised her teacher, Mr. Frank Herschberger, when she completed his assignment on "American Heroes." Miss Gordon chose an unlikely subject: women baseball players.

No such thing, you say? You'd be in the great majority, unaware of such luminaries as Toni Stone, Sophie Kurys, or Maud Nelson. Spend five minutes with young Miss Gordon, though, and she'll set the record straight. Miss Gordon conducted interviews, wrote letters, and dug deep into the musty reaches of the library's archives to learn about dozens of gals who made their living on the diamond, from the Gay '90s to the present day.

Miss Gordon, a talented pitcher herself, had some pretty strong opinions about why she thought her project was important: "Women have always been a part of baseball history, only it's a part that didn't get written down as much, so people have forgotten. Baseball is our national game, and this is the land of equal opportunity. I don't think these players got a fair shake."

Thanks to star student Katy Gordon, they're getting a second chance at fame.

The bell rang. I folded up the paper until it was the

size of a magazine, with the bottom half of page 17 at the front. When Current Events started, I raised my hand. Mr. H called on Linda Gallo first. She held up a headline about Elvis Presley joining the army.

"Not real *news*, Linda," Mr. H said, shaking his head. I heard a lot of sighs as half the hands in the room went back down. He looked around. "Katy," he said. "What do you have to contribute?"

"This is today's *Berkeley Gazette*," I said, holding it up. "I'm on page seventeen."

"I don't understand." He frowned. "You're reading the entire paper, and that's as far as you've gotten?"

"No, on page seventeen, there's an article *about* me. And you," I added quickly.

"Me?" Mr. H looked puzzled. He walked back to my desk. "May I see that?"

I handed him the paper. I watched as he read: his eyebrows shot up, wrinkling his forehead, and he started to smile. "That's quite impressive, *Miss* Gordon."

Now every kid in the class was staring at me.

"May I read this to the class?" Mr. H asked.

"Sure." I'd thought about doing that, but it had felt a little weird, like bragging.

He stood by the wall and read the whole article out loud. When he was done, there was silence. Sherm raised his hand. "Are you going to give her extra credit?"

Mr. H laughed. "I suppose I should." He put the paper down and gave a little speech about informed citizens being the key to democracy, and being involved in your community. After that we did vocabulary until the recess bell rang.

It was still drizzling, so nobody went outside. They all clustered around my desk, wanting to see the article. It was like I was famous. Pretty nifty. Mom would need to buy more copies. This one was getting a little ratty.

Mr. H asked if he could borrow it at lunchtime, to take to the teachers' lounge. "It's not every day that one of our students merits this sort of attention." It took half an hour to get home after school, because Jules had told *her* class, and everybody and their brother wanted to see. Then we went to my house to do our homework and maybe watch the afternoon movie, if it was Tarzan or the Three Stooges, not some dopey love story.

Her mom must have called mine, because there was a stack of *Gazette*s about a foot tall on the dining room table.

Mom made a list. One for Gramma Weiss, one for Suze, one for Aunt Babs, and a couple to mail to my dad and Dewey. I wanted one for my scrapbook, and one to send to Little League. Mom said she'd buy some frames, and hang one in her campus office and another on the dining room wall. She said she'd get a couple laminated, like her driver's license, so we could show them around without them getting wrecked.

We cleared a space on the table. Jules and I drank Cokes while Mom used her good scissors to cut out a dozen neat little rectangles. She put them into a file folder and looked at the clock.

"This calls for a celebration, don't you think?" She phoned Mrs. Berg, and an hour later the five of us piled into the Bergs' station wagon. We drove all the way to Spenger's, down by the bay. It was pretty fancy, with white tablecloths and waiters in red jackets. I had fried clams and a Shirley Temple in a real cocktail glass, with extra cherries.

My big news got smaller after a couple of days, then it wasn't *news* anymore. Everyone had heard. Except Little League. I taped one clipping to a piece of Mom's stationery, then sat down and wrote them a long letter. I told them I had proof that girls *had* played baseball—for more than fifty years—so there was no reason why I couldn't play on one of their teams. I reminded them that I *had* made the team, and asked them to reconsider their decision. I paper-clipped the copies of my report to the last page.

I went to the post office and stood in line, because I didn't know *how* many stamps the big fat envelope would need. Wow. More than a whole week's allowance? I hoped it was worth it. The 1958 Little League season started in a couple of weeks, so I also hoped they'd answer fast.

It was finally spring, but the ground was mucky from rain and we still couldn't play baseball. Recess was inside every day, dodgeball or kickball in the gym, so at least we got to run around.

Ten days later, I heard back from Little League. Another thin white envelope. This time I just ripped it open. They had to say yes. I'd given them enough ammunition to blow holes in *fifty* arguments. But they didn't. More of the same bull pucky. Girls are not eligible, it's a boys' game—blah, blah, blah. I didn't think they'd even *read* my letter, until I saw the last paragraph.

> We are always pleased to see young people take an interest in baseball history, and have reviewed your information. The next meeting of our Board of Directors is scheduled for October 19, 1959, at which time we will discuss any changes to Little League regulations. If you would like to submit a proposal to modify Section III, paragraph G, it will receive due consideration at that time.

1959? I'd be in junior high by then. Worse, I'd be twelve, and too old to play, unless they changed *all* their rules.

After everything I'd learned about women and baseball rules, I wasn't completely surprised by the letter.

Still, deep inside me I'd held out a tiny bit of hope, and now even that was gone. I was never going to play Little League. I sank onto the couch like all the air had gone out of me. After a couple of minutes I punched a pillow, and since Mom wasn't home, I yelled a bad word—loud—and punched it again.

Then I sat up and read the letter one more time. Still bull pucky. I started to crumple it up, but stopped before it was more than a little wrinkly. They were so wrong that someday they'd realize it and *have* to let girls play. Then this letter would be a piece of baseball history, too.

I went upstairs and pasted it to the last page of my scrapbook.

◇ ◇ ◇

A couple days later, Jules and I were up in the attic, playing a game we called Fastest Gun in the West. She had marbles and I had ball bearings, and we dropped them into the funnels at the top of the Wall and had a race to see whose hit the bucket at the bottom first. Extra points if one hit a xylophone bar.

Downstairs, the phone rang.

I flipped open two of the little gates, to set my path. "On your mark," Jules said, her finger on the trigger that emptied the left-side funnel. "Get set—"

"Katy! Phone!" Mom's voice boomed through the intercom.

I took my finger off my trigger. "Coming!" I looked at Jules. "Be right back."

The attic stairs were narrow and steep. Once I hit the upstairs hall, I ran to Mom's office and picked up her desk phone. "Hello?" I heard a click as Mom hung up in the kitchen.

"Kathleen Gordon?" a man's voice asked. I didn't recognize him.

"I'm Katy."

"Hi there. I'm Nick Winters. I'm a sportswriter for the *Gazette*."

Another interview? That was exciting. "What can I do for you, Mr. Winters?" I tried to sound grown up.

"Heh. I think it's more what I can do for *you*. Ralph Berg told me about the work you did. Fascinating, really fascinating. He says that you're a pretty good hurler yourself."

"In my neighborhood, sure."

"I started out in the sandlot myself," he said. "Ralph said you have interviews, photographs, letters. That's solid investigative reporting. Ever considered being a journalist? Sportswriter, maybe?"

"I hadn't really thought about it."

"Fair enough. How'd you like to try being a cub reporter for a day?"

"Like come to your office and help you?"

"No. We'd be working in the field." He chuckled. "Literally. Seals Stadium. The Giants are meeting the press for photos all morning, before the big parade. Since you're the history buff, Ralph thought you might want to be there at the start of a new era."

"Wowza!" I was so excited I could barely talk. "When?" I croaked out.

"Monday the fourteenth. I'd pick you up at nine o'clock sharp."

I felt my heart sink all the way down to my socks. "I can't. I have school."

He laughed. "Already cleared that hurdle with your mother. Nice lady. She understood. And believe you me, you won't be the only kid playing hooky *that* day."

"Okay then." I thought for a second. "What should I wear?" I crossed my fingers he wasn't going to say "school clothes," or "a nice dress."

"Pants you can shag balls in," he said. "You might get lucky. Oh, and bring your glove. I've met Willie Mays before. I think I can get you an autograph."

Chapter 30

Say Hey!

Sunday night, I was too excited to sleep. I climbed out of bed when it was light enough to see and got dressed: a long-sleeve shirt under my Seals jersey, my cleanest blue jeans, my high-top sneakers, my cap. Downstairs, I made myself toast and orange juice, quietly, so I didn't wake Mom. I paced around the kitchen, waiting, and around 8:00 I went outside to pitch.

There were still a few puddles, but the grass wasn't spongy anymore. I took the cover off my bucket of balls and untied the tire so it swung out from the tree. I lobbed a few easy ones through the center, then found my rhythm and started to really throw—a fastball, a curve, and my knuckleball.

I picked up another ball. A car pulled into the drive-way as I finished my windup, nice high leg kick, and threw a knuckler that bobbled right through the center of the tire.

Behind me, I heard a long, low whistle. "*Sweet* pitch," a man said as he got out of a red Chevy convertible. He was stocky and blond, younger than my mom, with a checked sports coat over a shirt and tie. "I'm Nick Winters. Mind if I see that one again?"

"Sure." I got the last ball out of the bucket, found my grip, and let it fly. That one had almost no spin at all, just fluttered through the tire and dropped to the ground on the other side.

"Ralph was right," Mr. Winters said. "You're one heck of a pitcher." He shook my hand, then helped me fill the ball bucket again.

Mom came out and moved to give me a kiss goodbye, then remembered—there was a *sports* person watching—and patted my shoulder instead. "Have a great time, sweetie. Aunt Babs says to tell you she's *very* jealous."

We drove with the top down, all the way across the Bay Bridge. Puffy clouds floated high in the sky, and sailboats glided out on the water. A perfect day. Mr. Winters and I talked about baseball. My favorite Seals player, Albie Pearson, had made it to the majors, as a Washington Senator. That's an American League team, so I wouldn't get to see him play, but I was glad for him.

We parked a block away from the ballpark. It had been repainted, a deep, dark green. The marquee still said SEALS STADIUM.

"Are they going to change it to GIANTS, before tomorrow?" I asked.

"Nah. They're only playing one season here, while the new park is built, down on Candlestick Point, so they left the name alone. A bridge between the past and the future, you know?"

He showed his press pass to a guard, and we went inside. It was all so familiar, and different. The building hadn't changed, but the colors had—black and orange everywhere, pennants that said GIANTS, a new logo. It was like seeing an old friend in disguise.

We walked up the vomitory—Mr. Winters laughed when I said the word—and I was even more surprised by the field. There was a whole new bleacher section in left—2,600 more seats, the paper had said—with red, white, and blue bunting hung *every*where.

I followed Mr. Winters down the steps, right onto the field. We were surrounded by Giants—big, muscular men in crisp black caps and bright white uniforms, no dirt, no grass stains yet, all smiling and joking. I was the shortest person there by about a foot, and it was hard to see, because all around the players were more men, in hats and suits and sports coats, every one of them with a notebook or a microphone or a camera. Flashbulbs popped every couple of seconds. The air smelled like melted plastic and the aroma of bread from the bakery across the street.

"I heard there are more than a hundred press guys here," Mr. Winters said. "Never seen coverage like it, not even for a World Series. It's definitely a milestone in baseball history."

Men stood three-deep around home plate. We walked down the third-base line a little and watched as players lined up for photos, answered questions, posed with bats and gloves.

Over the PA system, a voice boomed out, "Parade cars leave in one hour. One hour, gentlemen." More flashbulbs popped. When I blinked, the sky seemed full of little turquoise dots.

"Psst. Look over there." Mr. Winters pointed. Willie Mays had stepped into the shade of the dugout overhang. He wiped his forehead with a handkerchief and drank from a paper cup. For the moment, he was alone. "Want to meet him?" Mr. Winters asked.

"Yes, please."

We stepped nearer. "Excuse me, Willie. Nick Winters. I've got a fine young pitcher here who'd like to say hello."

Willie Mays sighed, very soft, the way my mom does when she thinks she's going to get to sit down, but the phone rings. Then he smiled, like he'd switched on a light. "Hey, Nick." He leaned down. "Pleased to meet you, young man."

I didn't correct him. "Me too." I thought for a second. "I met a friend of yours a while back. Toni Stone?"

"Toni." Now the smile was real. "How's that ol' gal doin'?" His voice was soft, with a southern drawl.

"Okay. She misses baseball a lot."

"I'll bet." He looked at me, at my glove. "You pitch, then?"

"Yes, sir."

"Any good?"

It was my turn to grin. "No one in *my* neighborhood can hit me."

"That so?" He looked thoughtful, then picked up a bat. "We got ourselves a couple of minutes, and I'm tired of answerin' questions. Why don't you show me your Sunday pitch."

"That would be—" I didn't have any words. "Sweller than swell."

He smiled again and put a big hand on my shoulder. We walked over to home plate. Home plate. At Seals Stadium. My feet barely touched the ground.

"Valmy," Willie Mays said. "Give this young feller a ball and catch us a few while he warms up?"

The man with the number 7 on his jersey nodded. "Sure, Willie."

I caught the underhand toss and walked out toward the mound.

"How old are you?" Willie Mays called out.

"Ten. And a half."

"Yeah. Okay. Where's the Little League rubber?"

"Forty-six feet." I paced it out and stopped.

"Fair enough," he said.

Valmy Thomas—the Giants starting catcher!—got into his crouch and held up a mitt the size of a dinner plate. We tossed easy ones back and forth until my arm felt loose. I held on to the ball. "Good to go."

"Let 'er rip," said Willie Mays, leaning the bat on his shoulder.

So I did.

I turned the ball in my glove, finding the seams, setting it so it felt *right* against my fingertips, like I'd done a hundred times before. But this was *Willie Mays*. I took a deep breath to steady all the butterflies, then another. Now or never. I gave a high leg kick and a good release, no wrist snap, smooth as butter. The ball fluttered and floated right across the plate, waist high. Willie Mays was so surprised he didn't even swing.

Valmy Thomas's eyes went wide when the ball landed in his mitt with a soft *thump*.

"Strike one," said Mr. Winters.

Willie Mays shook his head. He stepped out of the

batter's box, tapped his bat against his cleats. "Let me see that one again."

The second knuckler bobbed and dipped and—just at the last second—curved down around his knees. But Willie Mays swung hard, and I heard a loud *crack!* Every hat and cap in the place tilted up to watch the ball streak across the sky and into the stands—just inches outside the white pole.

"Foul ball," said a man with a camera. I looked over at the on-deck circle, where a crowd of reporters and players had gathered.

"Strike two," said another.

"Three's a charm," said Willie Mays. He shuffled in the dirt, setting his feet, opening his stance a little, watching every move I made.

I took a long, slow breath, cradled the ball like it was my best friend, and threw. No spin, nice wobble, it crossed the plate level with the letters that spelled out GIANTS across his chest. Willie Mays swung—and missed.

For a few seconds, time stopped. Nobody moved. Everyone stared. Then I heard Mr. Winters say, "You just struck out Willie Mays, kid."

Willie Mays laid the bat down and walked out toward the mound. Halfway there, he doffed his cap to me. I grinned, from ear to ear, my face feeling like it might split in two.

"You gonna be one fine ballplayer someday," he said.

"Promise me you won't never be a Dodger?"

I laughed. "Cross my heart."

"Arm like yours, that's the future." He looked down at my Seals jersey. "But you still dressed in the past." He turned and motioned to an older guy in a suit. The man came over and nodded as Willie Mays whispered in his ear, then sauntered off toward the clubhouse.

Willie Mays asked about my knuckleball. I showed him how I held it, where the seams were, how I curved my fingers. Then the man in the suit came back with a white bundle in one arm. "Here you go, Willie."

"Thanks, Lefty." He turned to me. "You're too young to be an official batboy, son. But I'd be happy if you was to wear this." He held out a brand-new Giants jersey and cap.

"Jeepers. I mean—uh—I'd be honored." Flashbulbs went *pop! pop! pop!*, bright white against the sunny blue sky, as I took off my Seals jersey, revealing my white shirt underneath, and became a San Francisco Giants fan.

"What's your name?" a reporter shouted.

I almost said Casey. Almost. Then I thought about all the baseball *girls* whose names nobody ever knew, or nobody remembers.

"Katy," I said. "Katy Gordon." I took off my Seals cap. The breeze ruffled my hair. Short, but not boy-short.

"I'll be a monkey's uncle," Willie Mays said. He shook

his head, then laughed. "Miss Toni Stone, she be right proud of you, child."

I grinned and settled the black Giants cap on my head, listening to cameras snap all around me.

"Parade cars loading in fifteen," the PA announcer boomed out. "Start making your way to Bryant Street, everyone." Men closed their notebooks, gathered up coats and hats, headed for the exit.

Willie Mays stood on the infield grass, not moving. The parade would wait for *him*. "Valmy, toss me that ball," he said. "Nick, a pen?"

Nick Winters handed over his fountain pen, and Willie Mays rested the ball on the top of my cap and autographed it for me. Then a man in a suit called to him. Willie Mays gave me a little nod, then loped off toward the waiting cars.

Mr. Winters drove us to the parade, downtown. We watched from the windows of the *Examiner* offices, right at Third and Market. Hundreds of thousands of people lined the streets to watch the Giants roll by in convertibles, players' names on the sides of the cars. Ticker-tape rained down on everyone. Men in suits and kids in T-shirts held signs saying WELCOME, GIANTS in English and Spanish, Chinese, Japanese, and a few other languages I didn't know.

It was the biggest crowd I'd ever seen. I watched until the last straggler cars went by. Then I sat back and cradled the baseball in my lap, running my finger gently over the magical words in bold blue ink:

Katy, the Queen of Diamonds

1-2-3

Say Hey!—Willie Mays

Chapter 31

Passing It On

On Tuesday, April 15, 1958, the Giants and the Dodgers played the first major-league game—ever—on the West Coast. The Giants won, 8–0.

Mr. H let us talk a little about baseball in Current Events the next morning, before going on to the rest of the news. Dead Laika had finally come down, disintegrating with a glow like a falling star. Van Cliburn, a man from Texas, won a piano contest in Moscow. It was a big deal, because he beat all the Russians in their own city.

Jules would be happy about that. A piano player on the front page.

For a week or so, I checked the Sports section of the *Chronicle* for a picture of me pitching, but no luck. Too much else going on. Mr. Winters did send me an 8 x 10 photo of me standing next to Willie Mays. I put it in my scrapbook.

I'd let Jules and PeeWee and Chip see my ball, but I didn't take it to school. I *had* been playing hooky, and showing that off was a bad idea. Some boys might get jealous enough to fink. Besides, I didn't want the autograph ink to get worn off by a bunch of sweaty hands.

The last Saturday in April, I woke up a little after nine. I slipped into my jeans and pulled on my new jersey with GIANTS across the front, black letters outlined in orange. I'd worn it a couple of times, but only around the house, so it was still white and clean.

The colors seemed a little Halloween-y to me. I missed the red and black of the Seals—they'd been *my* team since I was a little kid—but I guess it's like one of Mr. H's sayings: "The more things change, the more they stay the same." Aunt Babs and I would still go to baseball games at Seals Stadium, but now the Giants were the home team.

Downstairs, I poured myself a bowl of cereal and read the comics, then the sports page. The Giants had beaten the Cubs, 2–0, on Friday. I thumped my glove to get the pocket the right shape, and put on my black Giants cap, the orange S and F twisted through each other like a pretzel.

"Game today?" Mom asked, looking up from the crossword puzzle.

"Until around two. Then I have to come home and put on clean clothes for Jules's recital." I shrugged. "We have a deal. She watches me play sometimes, and I watch her play sometimes."

"That's nice."

"Yeah. We stick up for each other." I folded the comics page. "There wasn't rain last week, so the lot won't be a mud bath. Andy said he'd be there at ten thirty." I stood up. "I hope somebody's learned how to catch."

"I thought PeeWee did that." Mom moved on to the Jumble.

"He's got a Little League game today."

"Oh." She put her pen down and looked at me over the tops of her glasses. "You okay with that? It must feel a bit strange."

I shrugged. "Yes and no."

Mom raised an eyebrow, the professor signal for "I want a longer answer."

"Well—" I drank the last of my milk. "He's got his own plans, and I'd be a crummy friend if I wasn't rooting for him, right?"

She nodded.

"And he says there are *lots* of rules. Not just for the game, but about bedtime and snacks and *every*thing. Still, it stinks that they won't let girls on the team." I put my bowl in the sink. "I *proved* I can play, and they didn't care. That's stupid wrong. I bet there are *lots* of other girls as good as me."

"Agreed."

"But, think about it. If I *was* in Little League, would I even *know* that?"

She looked at me and waited.

"Okay, remember what you said about consequences? Last fall?"

"I do."

"Well, I was p.o.'d that they wouldn't let me play. But if they *had,* I never woulda gone to the library and found Jackie Mitchell." I grabbed a napkin and wiped off my milk mustache. "Or met Toni Stone, and had my picture in the paper and all."

"You certainly educated me."

"*And* I got to pitch in Seals Stadium." I picked up my glove. "In front of a whole lot of news guys. PeeWee's not gonna get to do *that*."

"Plus, along the way, maybe you changed a few minds about girls and baseball?"

"Yep. Like you said. Different ways to fight."

"The status quo doesn't stand a chance." She smiled. "My mother used to say that if someone dared to put up a fence, Babs and I would either climb over it or knock it down. You're definitely one of the family." She kissed me on the cheek.

"Mom. I've got a game."

"Right. Go get 'em, tiger." She tugged on the brim of my cap.

I walked down Russell Street to the lot. I always felt taller in my cleats. They made a soft clattery sound on the sidewalk, much better than ordinary shoes. It was a great day to be outside—blue sky, flowers coming up on people's lawns, a few baby green leaves on the trees. Like the world was waking up again, and *any*thing might happen.

Mike and Sticks were already there, playing catch by home plate, waiting for more guys.

"Hey, Gordon," Sticks said. "How's the arm?"

"A little rusty." I put on my glove and we made a triangle, tossing the ball 'round the horn, not a lot of pepper. Warming up. Sherm and Whiz showed up about ten minutes later, and we started hitting fungoes—grounders and pop-ups—trying to find our rhythm after a couple of months mostly indoors.

Chip and Catfish came on their bikes, with Andy right behind them, his little brother in tow. "You all know Butchie," he said.

"How old *is* he?" Mike asked.

"Eight. I told him he prob'ly couldn't *play*, but if he shagged balls by the fence, we might let him try to hit one."

"Got to start somewhere," Catfish said. Little brothers were a pretty automatic *in*.

We matched fingers. Mike and I were captains. I was about to take Chip for my first pick when I noticed a kid in pigtails standing across the street, watching us. She wore blue jeans and Keds and a plaid shirt with the sleeves hacked off, a glove tucked under one arm.

When she saw me look at her, she waved, a little flutter, the way you do when you're not sure what's allowed and what's not.

Wonder what she wants? I held up my hand. "Just a sec, guys." I stepped onto the sidewalk and signaled the kid: *C'mere.*

Her eyes opened in surprise. She pointed to herself. "Me?"

Who else? I nodded and she crossed the street.

She stopped a few feet away. "You were in the paper, right? The girl baseball expert?"

"Yeah. I was."

"I thought so." She held out her glove. "Will you sign it for me? You're kind of my hero."

Wow. "Sure. I guess." I felt my face get warm. "You play?"

"Yeppers." Up close I could tell she was younger than me—maybe fourth grade. "I'm little, but I'm fast, so I'm pretty good at shortstop. I can catch, too."

By now all the boys in the lot were staring at us.

The girl glanced over at them and sighed. "Look, all my cousins are boys. I know how it goes." She made a face. "Those guys aren't gonna let me play. And even if they did, I'd be stuck out by the fence all afternoon. But that's okay. I just came to watch *you*."

I shook my head. "We already got a rookie in left field," I said. "What's your name?"

"Jeanine. My friends call me Beano."

"I'm Katy." I stuck out my hand.

She smiled. "I know."

"Oh, right." I laughed. "Well, I'm captain today, and I lost my catcher to the bigs. You wanna give it a shot?"

"Really?" She cocked her head at the boys. "Are *they* going to like that?"

"They're good guys. And I have first pick today." I slung an arm around her shoulder. "You're with me, Beano. Let's go play some ball."

MEET
☆☆☆☆ KATY'S ☆☆☆☆
HEROES

LIZZIE ARLINGTON

(Elizabeth Stroud)
1876–1919
Pitcher

Cincinnati Reds: 1893
Philadelphia Reserves: 1898
Reading Coal Barons: 1898

Elizabeth Stroud was born in the coal-mining town of Mahanoy, Pennsylvania, and was the first girl in the town to ride a bicycle. She played baseball and other sports with the local boys.

She went to play for the Cincinnati Reds, a Bloomer Girls barnstorming team, in the early 1890s, pitching under the name Lizzie Arlington, and was a teammate of Maud Nelson.

Lizzie is believed to be the first woman to sign a contract to play "organized" baseball, and the first woman to sign a minor-league contract. When she joined the Philadelphia Reserves in 1898, she was making the astounding salary of $100 a week. (A coal miner made about $7 a week.)

Hired as much for the publicity as her ability, Lizzie often came into the stadium in a carriage drawn by two

white horses, wearing her gray uniform with a knee-length skirt, black stockings, shoes with cleats, and a "jaunty" cap.

A newspaper article said:

> She plays ball like a man and talks baseball like a man, and if it were not for her dress, would be taken for a man on the diamond, having none of the peculiarities of women ball players.

For a while, she was known all over the country as "the most famous lady pitcher in the world." She played with the New York Athletic Club and the Reading (Pennsylvania) Coal Barons of the Atlantic League, and did exhibitions with some barnstorming teams before getting married and settling down in Philadelphia.

ALTA WEISS

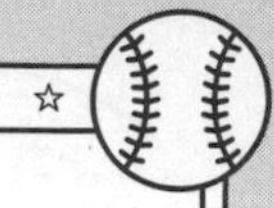

1890–1964
Pitcher

Vermilion Independents: 1907

Weiss All-Stars: 1908–1922

Alta Weiss grew up in Ragersville, Ohio, the middle daughter of a doctor. She played baseball with the neighborhood boys until she was in high school. When she was seventeen, the mayor of the town was so impressed with her pitching that he suggested that the manager of a semi-professional team, the Vermilion Independents, give her a tryout.

She struck out fifteen batters in her first game, and was allowed to join the team. As many as 3,000 people came to watch her pitch, some taking the train from 150 miles away just to see her. Hailed as the "Girl Wonder," she was a fan favorite and was frequently featured in local newspapers.

Her father built a heated gym so that she could practice in the off-season, and turned some nearby acreage into "Weiss Park," where she trained and played. In 1908, he bought a half interest in the Vermilion team

☆☆☆☆

and renamed it the Weiss All-Stars. Alta played in a black uniform. The men on the team played in white. They traveled throughout the Midwest, playing other semi-pro and minor-league teams.

She used the money she'd made from baseball to continue her education at Starling Medical College in Columbus (later known as The Ohio State University College of Medicine). She was the only female in the graduating class of 1914.

Alta joined her father's medical practice for a year, then worked as a doctor in a girls' reformatory, before taking over the office of another doctor when he went off to fight in World War I. She continued to play baseball most summers, finally retiring her glove in 1922, after more than fifteen years as a pitcher.

In 1925, she opened her own medical practice, and retired in 1948. Today her home in Ragersville is a museum dedicated to her baseball career, displaying equipment, scorecards, newspaper clippings, and other souvenirs of her playing years.

"Miss Weiss is no masculine girl, no tomboy. . . . She is no Amazon. . . . She threw the ball as straight as an arrow, and as fast, and when the catcher threw it back to her, it was no girly-girly toss ball, but a hot liner, which she caught."

—*Sandusky Star-Journal*, September 18, 1907

☆☆☆☆

LIZZIE MURPHY

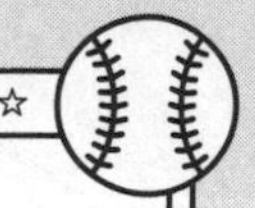

1894–1964

First Base

Providence Independents:
1911–1917

Ed Carr's All-Stars:
1918–1935

American League All-Star
Exhibition Game: 1922

National League All-Star
Exhibition Game: 1928

In her prime, Lizzie Murphy, also known as Spike Murphy, was billed as the Queen of Baseball, the best woman player in the country. She started her career at age fifteen, playing for amateur teams around her hometown of Warren, Rhode Island, before signing with the Providence Independents. From there she moved up to a nationally known barnstorming team, Ed Carr's All-Stars of Boston (sometimes called the Boston All-Stars).

The team played more than a hundred games a year, traveling all over New England and Canada. Lizzie wore a regulation uniform: a peaked cap, a wool shirt, baggy pants, and thick stockings with stirrups—with her name stitched across both the front and the back. That way the crowd knew that the player at first base was the woman they'd come to see.

☆☆☆☆

Lizzie supplemented her income selling postcards of herself between innings, sometimes making as much as $50 per game.

In 1922, the Boston Red Sox sponsored a charity game against some American League All-Stars. Lizzie played first base, becoming the first woman to play against a major-league team. In 1928, she played in a National League All-Star game against the Boston Braves, becoming the first person—of either gender—to play in both leagues.

After seventeen years of playing professional baseball, Lizzie Murphy retired in 1935.

Ed Carr said: "She swells attendance, and she's worth every cent I pay her. But most important, she produces the goods. She's a real player and a good fellow."

☆☆☆☆

MAUD NELSON

(Clementina Brida)
1881 – 1944
Pitcher, Third Base

Boston Bloomer Girls: 1897 – 1911
Western Bloomer Girls: 1911 – 1922
All-Star Ranger Girls: 1923 – 1934

For over forty years, Maud Nelson was active in every aspect of women's baseball. She pitched, played third base, scouted, and owned or managed many of the finest women's teams to play in the early days. In 1908, one reporter wrote that she was "the greatest all-around female ball player in existence."

In 1897, Maud was the starting pitcher for the barnstorming Boston Bloomer Girls. The team once won an amazing twenty-eight games in twenty-six days, and a Eugene, Oregon, paper said, "The girls from Beantown put up a clean game and play like professionals, asking for no favors, but playing a hard, snappy game on its merits."

Maud was the star attraction for the team, and had to pitch every day so as not to disappoint the fans. Often she would strike out the side for two or three innings, turn the ball over to the bullpen, and finish the game at third base, fielding grounders and rocketing bullets over to first base for another six innings.

When she was thirty, she became the owner-manager of the Western Bloomer Girls, in partnership with her husband, John Olson. She scouted both male and female players, dealt with booking agents, handled contracts, and managed the day-to-day operations of the team. Her husband died in 1917; six years later she remarried and, with her new spouse, Costante Dellacqua, formed the All-Star Ranger Girls, who played until 1934.

Wherever she traveled, Maud recruited the best of the local girls to play on her teams. Many of the finest female athletes in the early years of the twentieth century played either with her or for her. For three generations of women, Maud Nelson offered the opportunity of a lifetime—the chance to play professional baseball.

VIRNE BEATRICE "JACKIE" MITCHELL

1914–1987
Pitcher

Chattanooga Lookouts:
1931

House of David:
1933–1937

In the spring of 1931, Joe Engel, owner of the Southern Association's AA Chattanooga Lookouts, signed seventeen-year-old pitcher Jackie Mitchell. On April 2 of that year, the New York Yankees stopped in Chattanooga for an exhibition game, on their way home from spring training in Florida. A crowd of 4,000 came to watch, including scores of reporters, wire services, and even a newsreel camera.

Manager Bert Niehoff started the game with pitcher Clyde Barfoot, but after Barfoot gave up a double and a single, the manager signaled for Jackie Mitchell. The tiny rookie southpaw took the mound wearing a baggy white uniform that had been custom-made for her by the Spalding Company. The first batter she faced was Babe Ruth.

Jackie only had one pitch, a wicked, dropping curveball. Ruth took ball one, and then swung at—and missed—the next two pitches. Jackie's fourth pitch caught the corner of the plate, the umpire called it a strike, and Babe

☆☆☆☆

Ruth kicked the dirt, called the umpire a few dirty names, gave his bat a wild heave, and stomped out to the Yankees' dugout.

The next batter was Lou Gehrig. He stepped up to the plate and swung at the first pitch—strike one! He swung twice more, hitting nothing but air. Jackie Mitchell had fanned the Sultan of Swat and the Iron Horse, back-to-back.

A few days after that game, Baseball Commissioner Kenesaw Mountain Landis voided Jackie Mitchell's contract, claiming that baseball was "too strenuous" for a woman.

Crushed and disappointed, Jackie tried barnstorming, traveling across the country pitching in exhibition games. In 1933, when she was nineteen, she signed on with the House of David, a religious men's team famous for their very long hair and long beards. She traveled with them until 1937, but eventually got tired of the novelty and sideshow aspects of their games. (They once asked her to pitch from the back of a donkey.)

At the age of twenty-three, she retired and went to work in her father's optometry office, although she continued to play with local teams from time to time.

> "Her greatest asset is control. She can place the ball where she pleases, and her knack at guessing the weakness of a batter is uncanny. . . . She believes that with careful training she may

☆☆☆☆

soon be the first woman to pitch in the big leagues."

—*Chattanooga News,* March 31, 1931

"The Yankees will meet a club here that has a girl pitcher named Jackie Mitchell, who has a swell change of pace and swings a mean lipstick. I suppose that in the next town they will find a squad that has a female impersonator in left field, a sword swallower at short, and a trained seal behind the plate."

—*New York Daily News,* April 2, 1931

EDITH HOUGHTON

1912–2013
Catcher

Philadelphia Bobbies: 1922–1925
New York Bloomer Girls: 1925–1931
Hollywood Girls: 1931
Philadelphia Phillies (scout):
1946–1952

Edith Houghton was only ten years old when she joined the Philadelphia Bobbies, a factory team made up of women, all of whom bobbed their hair short. "The Kid" was so small that she had to tighten her cap with a safety pin and use a penknife to punch new holes in the belt of her uniform pants.

But Philadelphia sports reporters consistently praised both her hitting and fielding—at one time or another she played every position on the field.

In 1925, the Bobbies toured Japan, playing men's college teams for $800 a game. As a team they were less than spectacular, but the Japanese press had only good things to say about Edith.

When they returned home, Edith left the Bobbies to play for a number of women's teams, including Margaret Nabel's New York Bloomer Girls. She played one season

for the Hollywood Girls, making $35 a week playing men's minor-league teams.

In the mid-1930s, baseball opportunities for women disappeared with the demise of the Bloomer Girls teams, and Edith turned, reluctantly, to softball, playing for the Roverettes in Madison Square Garden. When World War II broke out, she enlisted in the U.S. Navy's women's auxiliary, the WAVES, and played on their baseball team as well.

After the war, Edith wrote to Bob Carpenter, owner of the Philadelphia Phillies, asking for a job as a scout. Carpenter looked through her scrapbook and decided to give her a chance, making her the first female scout in the major leagues. Edith scouted for the Phillies for six years before being called up by the Navy during the Korean War.

MILDRED ELLA "BABE" DIDRIKSON ZAHARIAS

1911–1956
Pitcher

Philadelphia Athletics: 1934
St. Louis Cardinals: 1934
House of David: 1934

Babe Didrikson was the greatest female athlete of the twentieth century, competing in baseball, basketball, tennis, golf, and track and field.

Called "Babe" after Babe Ruth because of her baseball ability as a girl, she became world-famous when she won two gold medals and a silver in the 1932 Olympics—in javelin, hurdles, and high jump. (She qualified for five sports, but women were only allowed to compete in three.)

In the spring of 1934, she pitched in an exhibition game for the Philadelphia Athletics (American League), then pitched in a spring training game for the St. Louis Cardinals (National League). That summer she joined the male barnstorming team, the House of David, and in an exhibition game, struck out New York Yankees slugger Joe DiMaggio.

The Cardinals pitching coach, Burleigh Grimes, said of Babe: "She would be one of the best prospects in baseball, if she were a boy."

Since there was nowhere for Babe to play professional baseball, she turned to golf, winning more than eighty tournaments. She was the only woman to make the cut in a regular PGA Tour event, and qualified for the U.S. Open, but her application was rejected on the grounds that the event was for men only.

She was the first female athlete to appear on the front of a Wheaties cereal box.

Babe's popularity exploded the myth that women could not be sports heroes, and her success mocked the idea that women could not compete because of their physical limitations. She opened the door for countless girls to have the opportunity to play professional sports.

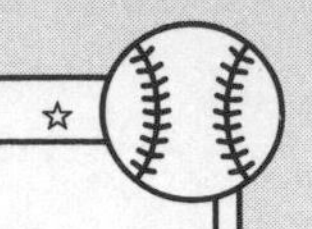

SOPHIE KURYS

1925–2013
Second Base

Racine Belles:
1943–1950

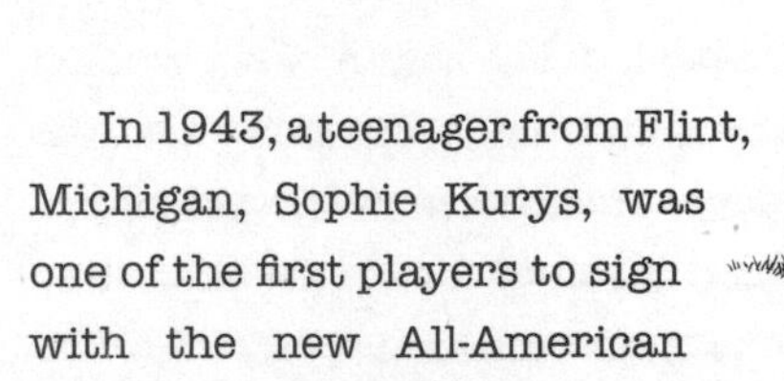

In 1943, a teenager from Flint, Michigan, Sophie Kurys, was one of the first players to sign with the new All-American Girls Baseball League, playing for the Racine (Wisconsin) Belles. That first season, the eighteen-year-old, known as the Flint Flash, was the team's left fielder and stole 44 bases. The next season, she moved to second base, where she played in 116 games and stole a league-leading 166 bases (out of 172 tries). But she was just warming up.

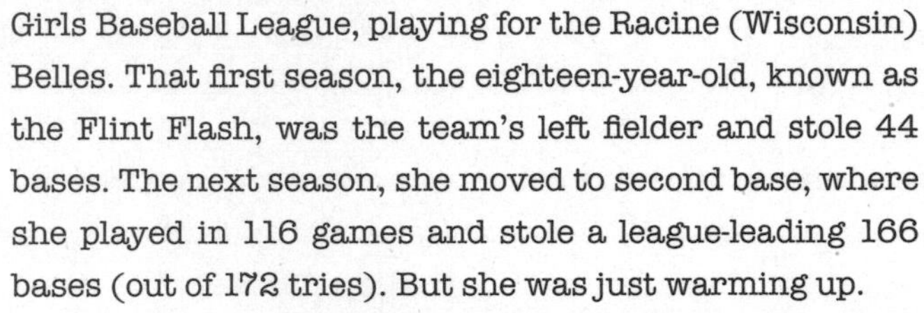

In 1946, she was voted the league's Player of the Year for her amazing athletic performance. In 113 games, she had 112 hits, scored a league-leading 117 runs, batted .286 (the second-highest average in the league that year), and had a phenomenal .973 fielding percentage at second base.

She also stole 201 bases (out of 203 tries). That's a record unequaled anywhere in professional baseball. Lou Brock held the men's record of 118 stolen bases in a season until Rickey Henderson broke it in 1982, stealing 130 that year.

And Kurys set that stealing record in a skirt. That's

not an insignificant detail. When a runner like her slid into second, she did it with bare legs. Sliding across the hard-packed dirt of the infield resulted in huge bruises and multiple "strawberries"—broken skin that often bled through the players' uniforms.

Kurys said, "The year I set the record, my chaperone made this donut affair so the wound wouldn't leak onto my clothes, because if it did, it would be torture to try to get the clothes off. . . . I had strawberries on strawberries. Sometimes now, when I first get up in the morning, I have problems with my thighs."

Despite that, Kurys stole a league-record 1,114 bases in the eight seasons she played for the AAGBL. (Only Rickey Henderson, who stole 1,279 bases in twenty seasons of play, has a higher career total.)

Sophie's feats didn't go unnoticed in the wider world of baseball. The 1947 yearbook, *Major League Baseball: Facts, Figures, and Official Rules*, featured Stan Musial on its front cover, and Sophie Kurys on the back cover.

DOROTHY KAMENSHEK

1925–2010
First Base

Rockford Peaches: 1943–1952

Dottie Kamenshek is considered by many to be the best female baseball player ever.

She played in the All-American Girls Baseball League for ten years, beginning in its very first season. She was named an All-Star in seven of those seasons. In 1946, she was the league's top hitter, batting .316. In her career, she struck out only 81 times in 3,736 at-bats.

Wally Pipp, a former New York Yankee, called her the most accomplished player he'd ever seen—man or woman—and predicted that she would be the first female player in the major leagues.

She was recruited by a men's team in Fort Lauderdale, Florida, but turned them down when she realized they wanted her as a publicity stunt, not for her baseball skills.

Kamenshek left baseball in 1952, and returned to school to become a physical therapist. She worked for Los Angeles County Children's Services until her retirement in 1980.

In 1999, *Sports Illustrated* named her one of the top

100 female athletes of the twentieth century. The character of Dottie Hinson in the movie *A League of Their Own* (1992) is largely based on Dottie Kamenshek.

> "She was the whole package. She could hit with power, or lay down a bunt and steal the base. She was a great first baseman—she could leap three feet in the air to grab the ball, or dig it out of the dirt. She was a tough lady, and as smart as they come."
>
> —"Pepper" Paire Davis, AAGBL catcher

ELEANOR ENGLE

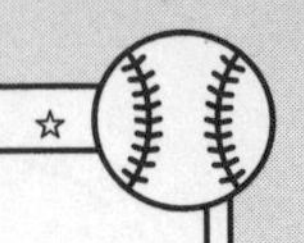

1926–2012
Shortstop

Harrisburg Senators: 1952

Eleanor Engle was a good ball player, but she is better known for the effect she had on women in baseball than for her skill. On June 21, 1952, she signed a contract with the Harrisburg (Pennsylvania) Senators, a minor-league farm team associated with the Philadelphia Athletics, as a shortstop.

The next day, in uniform, she practiced with the team, scooping up grounders and taking a few turns at bat. She did not play in the actual game.

Engle had been signed by the team president, Dr. Jay Smith. But the player-manager of the Senators, Buck Etchison, refused to allow her to take the field. "I won't have a girl play for me," he said. "This is no-woman's land, and I mean it."

The president of minor-league baseball agreed. He voided Engle's contract the following day and declared that "the signing of women players will not be tolerated, and clubs signing, or attempting to sign, women players, will be subject to severe penalties." Ford Frick, the commissioner of major-league baseball, made a similar statement.

In June of 1952, women were formally banned from playing professional baseball, and sixty-six years later, no woman has broken the barrier set up to stop Eleanor Engle from playing the game she loved.

TONI STONE

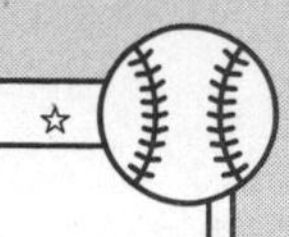

(Marcenia Lyle Alberga)
1921–1996
Second Base

San Francisco Sea Lions:
1949

New Orleans Creoles:
1949–1952

Indianapolis Clowns:
1953

Kansas City Monarchs: 1954

Toni Stone may be the best ball player you've never heard of.

As a teenager she played with the local boys' teams in St. Paul, Minnesota. During World War II she moved to San Francisco, playing first with an American Legion team, and then with the San Francisco Sea Lions, a black, semi-pro barnstorming team. She drove in two runs in her first at-bat.

She didn't feel that the owner was paying her what they'd originally agreed on, so when the team played in New Orleans, she jumped ship and joined the Black Pelicans. From there she went to the New Orleans Creoles, part of the Negro League minors, where she made $300 a month in 1949.

In 1953, Syd Pollack, owner of the Indianapolis

Clowns, signed Toni to play second base, a position that had been vacated when Hank Aaron was signed by the Boston Braves. Toni became the first woman to play in the Negro Leagues.

The Clowns had begun as a gimmick team, much like the Harlem Globetrotters, known as much for their showmanship as their playing. But by the 1950s they had toned down their antics and were playing straight baseball. Although Pollack claimed he signed Toni Stone for her skill as a player, not as a publicity stunt, having her on the team didn't hurt revenues, which had been declining as young black players joined the major leagues.

Stone recalled that many of the men shunned her and gave her a hard time because she was a woman. "They didn't mean any harm, and in their way they liked me. Just that I wasn't supposed to be there. They'd tell me to go home and fix my husband some biscuits, or any damn thing. Just get the hell away from here."

The team publicized Toni Stone in interviews, on posters, and on the cover of the Clowns' program. She appeared in fifty games in 1953, and hit .243. In 1954, Pollack sold her contract to the Kansas City Monarchs, an all-star team that had won several pennants in the "Colored World Series."

She played the 1954 season for the Monarchs, but the Negro Leagues were coming to an end, so she retired at the end of that season.

In 1990, Stone's hometown of St. Paul, Minnesota, declared March 6 Toni Stone Day. St. Paul also has a field named after her, located at the Dunning Baseball Complex.

She was inducted into the International Women's Sports Hall of Fame in 1993 (and is the only female baseball player there). She is honored in two separate sections in the National Baseball Hall of Fame in Cooperstown, New York: the "Women in Baseball" exhibit and the Negro Leagues section.

MAMIE "PEANUT" JOHNSON

1935–2017
Pitcher

Indianapolis Clowns: 1953–1955

Mamie Johnson was born in South Carolina. She lived with her grandmother, and played baseball with the boys in the neighborhood. When her grandmother died, Mamie went to live with relatives in New Jersey.

She was only allowed to play softball in school, but talked the local Police Athletic League into letting her pitch for their sandlot baseball team. She was their first girl and first black player.

"I didn't pitch like a girl," she said. "I had a surefire, windup, coming-right-at-you pitch, smack dab over the plate."

After high school, she wanted to try out for the All-American Girls Baseball League, but was not even allowed on the field because it was a whites-only league. Instead, she played on a Washington, DC, recreational-league team, where she was spotted by a former Negro Leagues player. He told her that the Indianapolis Clowns were holding tryouts.

Mamie went and pitched against their best hitters (including Toni Stone) and was signed that afternoon, the first woman to pitch in the Negro Leagues.

Mentored by the legendary Satchel Paige, she became known as "Peanut" because at 5'3" she was "no bigger'n a peanut." She played for the Clowns for three years, batting .273, with a win-loss record of 33–8.

When the Negro Leagues ended, she went to college and got a nursing degree, and worked as a nurse until she retired.

In 1999, Mamie Johnson created the They Played Baseball Foundation, dedicated to educating young people about the history of the game, and especially about the contribution of the Negro Leagues. She is also in the Hall of Fame in Cooperstown, in both the Negro Leagues section and the "Women in Baseball" exhibit.

AUTHOR'S NOTES

Although Katy Gordon and her family and friends are fictional characters, the women baseball players she discovers are quite real.

Until the movie *A League of Their Own* came out in 1992, most people had no idea that women had ever played professional baseball. Now *that* league is famous, but the rest of the history of women's baseball is still largely unknown.

The first recorded baseball game played by women was in 1866, at Vassar College. The first professional game—where fans were charged admission and players were paid—was in 1875, in Springfield, Illinois, between the Blondes and the Brunettes. Women continued to play pro ball for the next seventy-five years. But at the beginning of the twentieth century, men's professional baseball was becoming a multimillion-dollar business, and as it became America's national sport, it also became known as a man's game.

The history of women's baseball was ignored, erased, and gradually forgotten.

In 1950, a girl named Kathryn Johnston cut off her long braids, put on a baseball cap and blue jeans, and tried out for the Little League team in Corning, New York, along with her brother. She called herself Tubby, after a favorite comic-book character. She made the team. After a few games, she told her coach that she was a girl; he didn't care, because she was such a good player. But some of the boys' parents did care, and contacted the national Little League organization.

Up to that point, there was no rule about girls playing, because it hadn't occurred to anyone in the organization that a girl would *want* to play. So in 1951 they made one: "Girls are not eligible." It was nicknamed "the Tubby rule," and stayed in effect for twenty-three years.

What changed?

In 1972, then-president Richard Nixon signed a law called Title IX, which banned discrimination based on gender in any educational programs that received federal funding. It was a wide-ranging law, but is best known for its impact on college athletics. Before Title IX, only 1 percent of college athletic budgets went to female sports. Afterward, there was a 600 percent increase in women playing.

Title IX did not directly affect Little League, because it was not a federally funded organization. But it did open the door for female athletes.

In 1973, a girl named Maria Pepe was a player on a Little League team in New Jersey. She pitched three games before the national organization threatened to revoke the team's charter unless it removed Maria from its roster. *Girls are not eligible.*

But the National Organization for Women (NOW) contacted Maria's family and asked them if they wanted to fight. They did. NOW filed a lawsuit. Sylvia Pressler, hearing examiner for the New Jersey Division on Civil Rights, said, "The institution of Little League is as American as the hot dog and apple pie. There is no reason why that part of Americana should be withheld from girls."

Little League appealed the decision, and the case went all the way to the New Jersey Supreme Court. It took two years, but in the end, Little League had to change their rules and allow girls to play. (Maria was too old to play by the time the case was finished, but in 2004 she threw out the first pitch at the Little League World Series.)

Little League began accepting girls in 1974.

Katy Gordon would have been twenty-seven years old by then.

The next year, more than 30,000 girls signed up for Little League, and since then, more than ten million girls have participated in Little League programs. In 2018, one out of every seven Little League players is a girl. Most of them play softball, not baseball.

With a few notable exceptions.

Since 1947, Little League Baseball has held a World Series at its stadium in Williamsport, Pennsylvania. In 2014, Mo'ne Davis became the eighteenth girl (the fourth American girl) and the first African American girl to play in the Little League

World Series. She pitched a shutout game, 4–0, becoming the first girl to win a game in the Series, and the first to pitch a shutout. She then became the first Little League player—ever—to appear on the cover of *Sports Illustrated* magazine.

But there are still no women playing in the major leagues.

Eleanor Engle's contract was voided in 1952, and women were formally banned from playing in the majors or the minors. Since then, although there *have* been a few women who have played for independent minor-league teams, none have been signed to major-league-affiliated farm clubs. Some sources do claim the ban was lifted in 1993, when Ron Schueler, the manager of the Chicago White Sox, chose his daughter, Carey, in the forty-third round of the baseball draft. But she never actually signed a contract or played in a game.

As of 2018, the no-women ban has never officially been broken.

Women have a long history of playing baseball—more than 150 years. It is my great hope that one of the girls reading this book will be the pioneer who changes its future.

— Ellen Klages, July 2017

GLOSSARY

All-Star Game—a game that showcases the talents of the best players from many teams; the outcome of the game does not count as part of the rankings of the regular season.

Barnstormers—teams that operate outside an established league, traveling to various locales to play exhibition games.

Communism—a political system in which individual people do not own land, factories, or machinery. Instead, the government owns these things. From 1945 to 1990, the clash between Russian Communist beliefs and American capitalist values formed the basis of an international power struggle (the Cold War), with both sides vying for world dominance.

Curve—a pitch that curves away from a straight or expected path on its way to home plate (also: curveball).

Exhibition game—a sporting event whose outcome does not affect the team's record (also: pre-season game, charity game).

Fan—to strike a batter out, especially on a swinging third strike.

Farm team—a minor-league team that provides experience and training for young players; some (but not all) are affiliated with a major-league organization.

Fungo—a ball hit as practice for fielding; a ball tossed a short distance in the air by a batter, who then hits it.

Knuckleball—a pitch thrown with little or no spin that tends to flutter and move erratically toward the batter (also: knuckler, flutterball, floater).

Major League—the highest level of professional baseball, consisting of the National League and the American League (also: MLB).

Minor League—a professional baseball organization whose teams compete at a level below MLB. Some minor-league teams are affiliated with major-league clubs; some are independent.

Semi-pro—a team whose players receive some payment for playing, but which does not provide full-time occupation, such as factory teams or town teams.

Sinker—a fast pitch that has significant downward and horizontal movement and is known for inducing ground balls.

Slider—a fast pitch with a slight curve in the opposite direction of the throwing arm.

Spring training—workouts, practices, and exhibition games played before the opening of the regular season; generally mid-February through early April.

RECOMMENDED READING

Ackmann, Martha. *Curveball: The Remarkable Story of Toni Stone.* Lawrence Hill Books, 2010.

Dickson, Paul. *Sputnik: The Shock of the Century.* Walker Books, 2011.

Gregorich, Barbara. *Women at Play: The Story of Women in Baseball.* Harcourt, Brace & Company, 1993.

Houts, Michelle. *Kammie on First: Baseball's Dottie Kamenshek.* Ohio University Press, 2014.

Krumm, Brian. *The Little Rock Nine.* Capstone Press, 2014.

Macy, Sue. *A Whole New Ball Game: The Story of the All-American Girls Professional Baseball League.* Henry Holt & Co., 1993.

Patrick, Jean L. S., and Ted Hammond. *The Baseball Adventure of Jackie Mitchell, Girl Pitcher vs. Babe Ruth.* Graphic Universe, 2011. (Graphic Novel.)

Vernick, Audrey. *The Kid from Diamond Street: The Extraordinary Story of Baseball Legend Edith Houghton.* Clarion Books, 2016.

Websites

The History Museum, South Bend, Indiana—historymuseumsb.org
Extensive material on the All-American Girls Baseball League.

National Baseball Hall of Fame—www.baseballhall.org
Includes a curriculum on women's baseball called "Dirt on Their Skirts," with downloadable lesson plans and resources.

Negro Leagues Baseball Museum—www.nlbm.com
Includes biographies of Toni Stone, Mamie Johnson, and Connie Morgan.

Sputnik beeps—To listen to the actual 1957 broadcasts from Sputnik, go to Google and search for "Sputnick beeps."

ACKNOWLEDGMENTS

Almost twenty years ago, when I worked for the Exploratorium museum in San Francisco, I created a website called "The Girls of Summer," part of an online exhibit on "The Science of Baseball" (www.exploratorium.edu/baseball).

Thanks to my then-boss, Ruth Brown, for giving me the opportunity to follow my curiosity and explore the history of women's baseball. (And thanks to David Barker for his wonderful online illustrations!) I had gathered a lot more fascinating material than I could use, and it sat in my files for many more years, until I decided to write this novel.

Thanks to the National Baseball Hall of Fame, the Negro Leagues Baseball Museum, the Northern Indiana Historical Society, and the Chattanooga Regional History Museum for the resources that started me on this journey. Thanks to Barbara Gregorich, Gai Berlage, Debra Shattuck, and Leslie Heaphy and Mel Anthony May for their invaluable books and extensive primary research. Thanks to the San Francisco Public Library, the Berkeley Public Library, *the San Francisco Chronicle*, and the Berkeley Historical Society for bringing the local past alive for me.

Sharyn November convinced me to write this book and, along with my agent, Jill Grinberg, helped to find it a home at Viking. *Out of Left Field* would not be what it is today without the careful reading, sage advice, and perceptive suggestions of my editor, Leila Sales. I am grateful for their encouragement and support.

Travel back in time with more award-winning historical fiction from Ellen Klages!

★ "An intense but accessible page-turner."

—*The Horn Book*, starred review

★ "First-rate historical fiction."

—*Publishers Weekly*, starred review

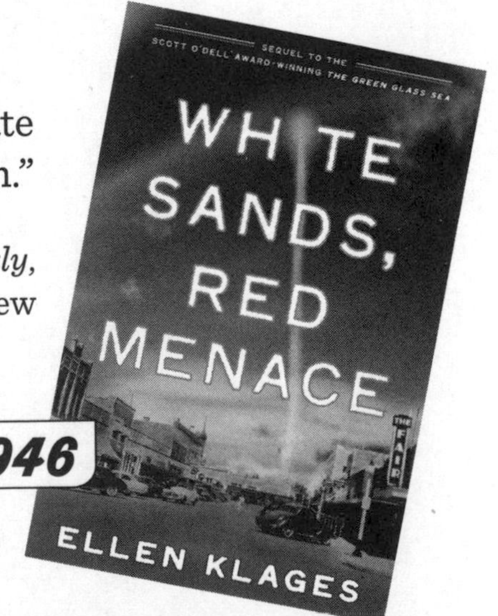